FALLEN FROM SHADOW…FOUND

A VAMPIRE ROMANCE…

FALLEN FROM SHADOW...FOUND IN GRACE

A VAMPIRE ROMANCE

BY: ANDREA DEAN VAN SCOYOC

©2006 – 2008

First Printed in North America 2007

Second printing of story with new title 2009

FORMATS:

Print ISBN: 978-1-4357-3646-7

E-Book

EDITING BY: Andrea Dean Van Scoyoc and Cannibal Rose

SPECIAL DEDICATION

To CANNIBAL ROSE of CANNIBAL ROSE CREATIONS…
http://www.cafepress.com/cannibalrose

THANK YOU for helping me breathe new life into this book.
You are greatly appreciated…

FALLEN   VAN SCOYOC

INTRO:

Twilight Innocent was always a special story to me. A tearjerker and a work of many hours of love, I don't feel that it was given the chance it deserves.

It saw such a short run in print the first time that few people had a chance to enjoy getting to know Farayne on her journey.

I am pleased to re-offer this manuscript with new editing, a new title and a fresh outlook.

It is my sincere hope that this book will attain the type of status and audience I had originally hoped for.

Thank you for giving us another chance…

DEDICATION:

To Nano Hayes…the first *Aggie*.

To my fans who have followed me through thick and thin, dark and light…my eternal love and gratitude…

Technical Information on the Anglican Church, courtesy of:

http://www.anglican.org/church/ChurchAdmin.html

TABLE OF CONTENTS:

CHAPTER ONE
AN ESCAPE

She watched the sky turn from pale black to pale gray. The sun would be rising within the next hour but she sat contentedly by her fairy fountain, surrounded by her beloved roses. She was utterly at peace.

Though no one would see it, she had chosen to attire herself in the beautiful gypsy-styled dress she'd recently found while out thrift shopping. There would be no need for pomp, no need for any goodbyes. This was how she wished to leave this earth and she wanted no tears shed.

She smiled as her mind's eye looked back on the many centuries of her life. It did indeed seem like so many lifetimes ago that she'd been an unhappy socialite and embarked on her journey. It had been the journey of a lifetime--a lifetime that had seen more happiness, pain, laughter and sorrow than a hundred lifetimes could hold.

Her mind took a trip back, even if only for a moment on what her life had been, had become and how it was slated to end...

The wind chilled her as she looked across the landscape that she called home. As beautiful as it was -- from the thick fog that blanketed everything in a quiet gloom at night to the rolling hills and bright green grass that beckoned anyone who wished to linger in its lush embrace during the day -- it still felt alien to her. She shivered and pulled her cape tightly about her. How she wished she could enjoy sanctuary...alone, with no one to bother her while she listened to the sounds of the shadows.

"There you are, my dear! Why did you leave the party? You missed my speech!"

She smiled gently. She cared nothing for her father's speeches, the same ones that he made repeatedly and she cared nothing for this gala...not tonight, not *any* night. She simply wanted to go home and walk the grounds of the estate where she could find some much welcome solitude. She'd been so tempted to sneak away...

"I apologize, Father. It was stuffy in the house. I simply needed to breathe some fresh air."

A kiss pressed against the top of her ebon head.

"I understand, my dear. You know these revelers love their pipes and drink. However, don't be very long out here. The night is chilly and I do not wish you to take ill in the dampness."

She managed as pleasant a smile as envisioning her return to the party would allow her.

"Of course, Father."

It was not the pipes nor was it the drink that bothered her. She actually enjoyed the tantalizing scent of burning tobacco; as for drink, though she did not imbibe herself, she faulted no one who did. In truth, it was the *company* in the house that she loathed.

She listened to make certain that her father had securely closed the balcony door and sighed in relief. Solace, that was all she sought. Was that so difficult to obtain?

Her name was Farayne Gleneden and she was very beautiful. A socialite of upper class and impeccable breeding, she had the type of life most other women could only dream of. Yet she was not happy and sadly, could not remember the last time she'd truly been so. The endless teas, gala affairs, tedious parties...and her father trying to push her off onto every young, handsome, available upper class man in London angered her and caused her much discomfort. She hated all of it.

She tired of seeing the same people each and every day, the people who pretended to be her friends, but who she knew secretly whispered about her behind her back. She longed for something different, something to give her life meaning. She longed for adventure. Adventure for a lady of her prominence was unheard of and she knew that the most adventure she could ever hope for would be if she lived through childbirth. However that was not the type of adventure she wanted. She wanted to help others not as privileged as she, she wished to travel…without her father; she wished to see forbidden things and learn ancient languages and customs. While she longed for true experience and knowledge she did not want just that which could be gained from books, but what living life itself could teach her.

She'd seen the beggars at the manor -- her manor -- Stoningham Green and how they'd been harshly admonished for pleading for food and water. Why had they been turned away? Her family had enough food to feed an army, yet they could not spare crumbs for hungry people; people whose faces showed hard times and sadness. The children were the worst, clinging to their parents, their famished eyes wild and terrified, not understanding why they were hungry and why the man at the gate, Theodorus the gatekeeper, was yelling at their parents.

Then her mind's eyes traveled to other things she'd seen that intrigued her, such as the women that her father would call witches, the women that those in town condemned. She heard the whispers when she traveled into town, which was not very often (as her father did not like her going there alone), but there were times that she had gone -- alone. The holy and prim and proper women all chattered the same, hushed and harsh about those *women* and how they engaged in things that were evil; things that were considered sinful. But *why* were the activities sinful and evil? *Who* decided that they were not of God? These were the things that Farayne also wished to learn about; customs *so* different from her own upbringing that people thought them evil or wrong.

She tried to clear her thoughts. This night she was a guest at yet another gala, another torturous affair that she would have all but sold her soul to get out of attending. All night she'd watched the people in attendance. She'd listened to the gossip of the girls of wealth and haughty nobility and how they made fun of the poorer members of society. In other areas of the house as she desperately tried to get away from their insidious laughter, she'd heard the men--how they talked of sport and the hunt and how much better they were than the men who tended their horses for them. All of it made her sick. Here they were happy and laughing, oblivious to anything but their own greed and pleasure, when there were members of society who could benefit from an education and tutelage in fine arts. Did those arrogant fools actually think that the forlorn and forgotten dregs they so casually laughed about, wished to be in the waste their lives had become?

Why not devote time to helping them see fruition from their pathetic existence instead of focusing on such trivial things as what type of fabric one's clothing was made out of or how much one paid for his pipe or her dress?

She would leave this party early. She had to. She didn't know how much more she could bear. Her father had introduced her to yet *another* single fellow socialite, Ronan Tanserlyn, the local well-to-do heir of London's largest lumber company. Her father, Dashen, had grown up with Ronan's father, Airk, and they'd been friends their entire lives. Farayne would do nothing to damage her father's standing in the community or his friendship with Airk, but she didn't think highly of Ronan. She considered him to be self-deluded, conceited, egotistical and boring. She'd spoken with him briefly only to placate her father, then managed to slip away. Her suitor's idea of conversation was how wonderful she looked, how well-groomed and impeccable he was, and how much money and sustenance he could provide her as his wife, *if* she were smart enough to accept his proposal. That conversation left her nauseated. *If she were smart enough to accept his proposal?* He acted as if their marriage would be a business arrangement! Luckily, after she excused herself, she'd been able to avoid him for most of the night.

Her father's presumptions angered her. Why could she not pick her own husband? Not that she was interested in a husband yet; she had other things she wished to do before settling down. She'd only recently turned eighteen! Why did her father feel it necessary to control *every* aspect of her life? She did not even have a life so to speak and yet her father managed, much like he did his estate, every detail of her existence, even down to choosing *her* husband! He'd always been controlling but after her beloved mother's passing three years previously, he'd become downright intolerable.

She slipped out the side door of the manor and began the two-mile walk to Stoningham. She'd ridden in her father's carriage to the party, but she would miss the ride home. In actuality, she would not *miss* it. The walk would do her good and give her time to clear her head. She was angry and wasn't sure why. She should be *accustomed* to her father's meddling by now, but she simply could not become so complacent as to *accept* it. The same could be said for those she was forced to endure at the parties. Human behavior had always been bothersome to her but as she aged, she often found that it got worse instead of better and her tolerance for those who acted childishly became less and less. She looked up and allowed the damp air to cool her face. The night was beautiful; the moon was full and a gentle breeze rustled her cape. She wasn't as chilled as she had been earlier. Could it have been the company previously that made her shiver? She tossed her head and continued on her way hoping that this gala would be the last she would have to attend for a while.

She had a long walk ahead of her. As hard as she tried to concentrate on simply putting one foot in front of the other without falling into the puddles that riddled the road after the previous night's rain, she found that her mind wandered. It often did that and though at times it was comforting, this night it was not. She really needed to focus on getting home unsoiled, not taking a trip in her mind to another place…anything to escape where she was. The road was littered with tree branches and other debris -- and she was attired in one of her finest dresses. How would she explain to her chambermaid if she ruined it?

She huffed and rolled her eyes, dropping the clumsy and far too heavy dress hem from her tiny hands. So what if she ruined the dress? It was not like it was her only one. As she intentionally stepped into a puddle, she allowed her mind to wander. She was already angry and upset at the way the night had progressed, or more like digressed -- from the snotty looks she received from her peers as she walked in the door, to the loathsome men who vied for her hand.

Things had been so much simpler as a child. Of course, she did not remember her earliest childhood, but she did remember from about the age of five years, on.

She arrived screaming (literally her mother told her) into the world on a cold winter's day, December 22nd to be exact. The birth was a difficult one, one that left her mother weakened and near death -- also one that left her unable to produce any further children. Farayne's mother never *told* her that she blamed her for her inability to give her any siblings but still...

Farayne wouldn't even have known the particulars about her mother's failed health if one of the chambermaids hadn't told her. It wasn't that the woman was trying to be nasty or hurtful, she just believed in being honest. Farayne often asked the maids while growing up, as children are wont to do, when she was going to get a little brother or sister. The maids never would answer, so the child went to her mother. That black day was forever etched in her mind and haunted her no matter how hard she tried to forget it. Even as an adult she was not allowed to assuage the guilt over the hurt she'd caused her mother just out of curiosity. The first time it happened, the day that Farayne innocently asked when she'd get a playmate, the poor woman burst into tears and ran from the room. She chased after her mother, asking why she was crying. Her mother slammed her bedroom door right in Farayne's face and refused to open it back up. The door stayed closed, her mother inside, for three days. Her father never said anything to her although the child got the feeling that she'd done something very bad.

After that episode, there was always an uncomfortable feeling between the mother and daughter. It was the worst in the days after the crying fit but lessened as the nights passed. When her mother emerged from the room, she hugged her daughter, kissed her sweetly and then walked away. Farayne didn't speak, she did nothing, save for stand in the hallway and watch her mother simply walk away. It was obvious that the barren woman loved her daughter very much but from that day forward the beautiful child could never shake the feeling that she'd done something wrong and that she were to blame for *something*.

She was around ten years old when she finally got up enough courage to ask her maid as she bathed her one evening why she could have no brothers or sisters. It was then that she learned the truth as to why her mother behaved so irrationally when she asked her. The child cried pitifully as the old woman explained to her that she was to blame for wiping out her mother's womb and

12

leaving her barren for the rest of her days. The maid was careful to make certain that Farayne knew that her *parents did not blame her*, but that it *was her birth* that caused her mother to become infirm. The words seemed like a piece of poison fruit to the child. On one hand it was not really her fault that she couldn't have any brothers or sisters, but then again it was.

The maid went on to tell the child that her father was extremely disappointed in not being able to have a son, an heir to carry on the Gleneden name, yet that he too would never *openly* say a word. Farayne said nothing as the maid took her from the tub, toweled her dry and dressed her for bed. She stayed silent as the old woman read to her and then kissed her goodnight. Somewhere in her subconscious, as she was yielding to sleep's inviting threshold, she vaguely remembered her mother leaning over her to kiss her soft forehead.

She didn't sleep well that night.

In the days that followed, she paid close attention to her father's actions and reactions to her. Being armed with the maid's information gave her so much insight! Things had always felt strange in her home yet what was worse was the inability to understand why. She was a precocious child and although young in age, she was incredibly intelligent and observant. She'd always known that something was wrong in the Gleneden mansion. Now she knew what. She had to admit that although her father seemed to love her she could not help but feel his upset as well.

Unlike most children though, Farayne did not allow what she'd done to her mother to openly bother her. She was smart enough to realize that the body was imperfect. Although created in God's image, all one had to do was be injured to see that the human body was already weak and fallible. She had a scar on her knee from when she fell off the back steps of her home. The maids made a fuss over her and her mother dried her tears but she still had a large, ugly scar on her knee. Such inner working as the organs to produce a baby had to be much more complicated. If something a simple as falling down could cause such injury to the outside, what could stress and birthing another human being cause a body on the inside? Farayne was glad to learn, years later in school, that she'd been right. That helped her cope more so than anything.

Luckily she never had to see her parents all day, every day…especially her father. She never cared much for either parent's company -- it was not as if they went out of their way to spend a great deal of time with her when she were smaller -- although as her mother became sicker and Farayne became older, the two women spent quite a bit of time together. If her mother's love was an act, it was a good one. Life went on as if she'd been *chosen* to be the only child born. Her mother even fondly referred to her as her "Christmas baby."

Farayne wasn't certain if that was a ploy her mother invented to make herself feel better, but she said nothing, allowing the woman to live in a fantasy world if it helped her cope with her body's betrayal. One of the stories she liked to tell people was that before her darling daughter was born, when her father asked his beloved what she wanted for Christmas, with belly bulging, she stated that the only thing she wanted was to have a healthy baby. She got her wish. Weighing eight pounds and crowned with a shock of ebon hair, she was the pride of her parents.

Farayne would simply smile sweetly, appearing to drink in all of the kind words and cherished compliments that others gave the story. It sickened her, as she knew that her mother did not completely feel the way she portrayed herself to feel in the story, but they both had to do what was necessary for their own sakes.

One thing that she did have to admit though was that she had the best of everything growing up. She never wanted for anything. Her clothing was tailor-made out of the finest velvets and softest imported fabrics, her hair always washed with the best of shampoos and combed just so, her baths always scented and warm, her toys always the most expensive and her education one that would rival any king or queen's offspring.

Farayne shuttled her true feelings -- much the way she believed her mother did -- to the back of her mind and put on a good face, actually enjoying mother's company as the two of them lived their lives. But there was still something missing in her life. She had no idea why she felt that way but she did. She had the type of life that any young woman would give her soul to have and yet *something was missing* in her life…something that she could never put

her finger on. Though she and her mother would pick flowers --
when her health allowed -- they would bake, they would sing and
spend many happy hours knitting and embroidering none of it ever
made the young girl happy and she never felt complete.

    As the years passed, Farayne watched her mother's health
fail increasingly and her father become even more possessive,
guarded and interfering in all matters of their lives. He'd always
been a proud father but *doting* was *not* something he did. He admired
and loved his daughter from afar…unless he wished to control her
every move, which he often did.

    Farayne frowned as she remembered the day that her
father's meddling became so obvious to her that she felt as if her
life were unbearable. She was around fifteen years of age and she
thought she'd seen and heard everything that he could put her
through. She'd been invited to a mother-daughter tea. Her mother
was too ill to attend so she did what any self-respecting young
woman would have done. Without her mother to be at her side, it
would have been inappropriate to do anything but. Farayne sent the
invite back with a polite decline to the event. No young woman in
her right mind would dare attend a social gathering alone when the
invite specifically dictated that it was a mother-daughter event,
especially when that mother was bed-ridden. Farayne's father knew
the father of the young woman hosting the event, a powerful,
wealthy and influential banker and fearing that his opinion of him
would be tarnished and therefore hindering his chances of using
him to further himself if he needed to at some point, became
enraged that his daughter would dare send back an RSVP in the
negative. To add insult to injury, as the young woman did what she
did thinking that she was doing the right thing, he forced her to
personally go, by coach of course -- just because she was in trouble
did not mean that she had to travel like a commoner -- to the
banker's home, where the party was being held and apologize. Once
she'd apologized, she was to come right back home and get ready to
go, taking the same route to the party and explain to everyone there
why she'd tried to, incorrectly, get out of attending.

Farayne was incredulous! No young woman should have to endure such humiliation! She was innocent of treachery, as her father insisted that what she did was, and beseeched her mother for help. However the sickly woman was too weak and frail to fight her husband, whether with impassioned pleas or with genuine tears. She simply asked her daughter to go and appeal to the morality and social upstanding of the partygoers.

With a heavy heart Farayne did as her mother asked but she would never forget her shame -- and her burning face to match -- as she apologized to each mother and daughter in attendance, many of them her sworn enemies who'd shown past discourtesy not only to herself but to her mother as well, about her lapse in manners. On the way home that evening she sobbed her heart out and refused to speak to her father for three days. It was only at the intervention of her mother, getting out of bed to do so; Farayne was certain that her father was responsible for her mother visiting her in her room, that made the young woman speak to him again. Things were never the same between the two of them after that. Father and daughter grew even more distant until they were nearly complete strangers. She loved her father, as any dutiful child would, but just that small taste of power…and greed for more power was something that she would loathe and never forget.

It was then that she began to rebel…in her own way. She began spending more hours than ever outside, alone, she began picking flowers on her own, wandering miles from the manor, thinking, *dreaming* of the day that she would finally be free from her father's clutches. No matter how bad things were though, they could always be worse. She refused to sacrifice what small shred of peace and freedom she had for a husband that would hold her back, control her and dominate her life even more so than her father. She certainly was not going to give *anything* up for a man that she didn't love. She'd met no man she loved and doubted she ever would if the *boys* she'd grown up with were any indication.

Almost as if reading her thoughts, her father began introducing her to wealthy young men from neighboring towns that she knew nothing about. They were just as bad as the ones she'd grown up with. She wanted no part of them either and no part of any of their bravado.

FALLEN   VAN SCOYOC

Farayne became increasingly withdrawn into her own little world with each unwanted introduction, with each kiss of her hand and with each hollow compliment.

It wasn't long after her 16th birthday that her mother, weak, sick and simply a shell of the glorious and radiant beauty she'd once been, died.

The day started out like any other with the raven-haired girl up at dawn to watch the night give way to the morn. In her hand she held a biscuit smeared with tasty blackberry juice -- her favorite -- and hand-churned butter, the diligent work of one of the kitchen maids. She sat at the edge of the small pond on their property, the morning's mist embracing her in the beautiful chill. She pulled her thickly knitted, heavy shawl tighter about her. It was mornings such as the ones she was greeted with every day that she wished she could paint…somehow capture to cheer her when times seemed the roughest. The world was so quiet, asleep in its own cocoon, the fog swirling and the mist inviting her to explore within it, almost like out of some fairytale her maids had told her as a child. Everything was gray…gray and so calm. She expected any moment to see a handsome young man, long hair hanging below his shoulders, eyes set upon her as if she were a princess, come strolling out of the fog. "My darling…I have found you," he would say. She smiled. Oh if only it could happen like that. Instead, more often than not when her father insisted on introducing her to the young men that seemed to almost materialize from thin air, she was met with, "Greetings. It is my pleasure to meet you, although I am certain that you will find by the time the evening is over with my company to be just as pleasurable."

She rolled her eyes. Why was every man she ever met so engrossed in only himself? She strained her eyes at the swirling blanket before her as if willing her hopes to be realized. If only her dream man would come walking out of the fog, the early morning mist swirling at his feet, if only he were searching for her the way she'd been, and she was sure would, continue searching for him, she would be very happy. That would be one dream that she would give *anything* to see fulfilled.

Farayne would sit like that in her own little world for as long as the morning would allow her, drinking in the peace and quiet and listening to the birds as they awoke from their slumber. Then, almost imperceptibly, they would appear…like the fabled light from Heaven, the bright beams of sunshine that began piercing the darkened clouds. It would be one at first, then two and then a few more. It was as if they had an order to their appearance. They would each wait respectively until the other had a chance to be seen and settle itself into the proper place and then the next one would appear to find its place. They would settle beside her, in front of her…almost as if surrounding her, sheltering her from her father…giving her the safety that her mother could not.

Once the ethereal and warming beams of light turned into a blanket of heat, she would retreat into the woods to the cool and damp sights and smells she loved so much. The forest was a melancholy solace for her and she reveled in all that it offered her. She would inhale as much as her nostrils would allow and then breathe the clean and earthy air out, feeling almost as if she'd been renewed. She found paths to explore, watched the small and furry animals scurry about, wishing that she could touch one, to communicate with it somehow. She'd never been allowed to have a pet, save for the horses in the stable. But they were more of her father's and the stable boy's pets to groom, to coo over, to race, and to use as bragging rights to anyone who thought they had better modes of transport, than pets for her. She hugged the horses, she talked to them, she braided their tales when they allowed her to, she petted them, but she couldn't pick them up and cuddle them when she was sad. She couldn't bring them into the house…there were so many times that a small pet could help her through the dark and gloomy nights that threatened to swallow her up. Occasionally a beam of light would follow her into the glade, lighting her path or showing her a hidden treasure almost as if only she was to see it. She would stay in her wooded home until she became famished with hunger. It would be with aching steps and apprehensions clutching her heart that she returned to her house for only the simplest of food to nourish her, hoping that her father would not be there. Most of the time he would not be and that pleased her greatly. The times when he had been home for whatever reason, she would find potable food, whether it be an apple, a pear or some bread and then quickly run out of the house again.

It happened much that way the day that her mother died. It was Farayne who found her. Coming back from one of her long, solitary walks, she took an apple from the kitchen and started to go back outside when she decided to see her mother briefly.

Thankfully, her father was not home so she could spare a few moments. Surely her mother grew weary of speaking only with the maids who waited on her hand and foot, night and day.

She slowly ascended the steps, hoping to surprise her. She actually had two surprises for her, her visit and then something she wanted to tell her that she'd found while out that morning. Whilst out amongst the solitude of her forest, she'd seen a pretty flower sitting all alone in a shaft of sunlight. It was one of those times when the light seemed to have a purpose for her. That purpose was to show her that the brave fight not always with the largest of armies, but oftentimes alone, so alone, away from anything and anyone they knew. That flower symbolized herself in a way and also reminded her of her mother, alone in a world (or in her mother's case, a body) that she was no match for any longer, yet still beautiful and struggling to survive day-to-day. Farayne hoped that the moment would be a special one for them, one to remember as a good time in their lives and not the painful memories the lovely young woman had of the strained times and false fronts they'd put on to keep up the charade of the idyllic mother and daughter.

The top step creaked as she put her weight on it and she cringed. She waited a moment and then when she was certain that she could forge ahead, she did. She tiptoed into her mothers' room and kissed her forehead trying not to wake her. Her mother's head was cold. That was odd. The window was open and a warm but comfortable breeze was wafting into the room. How could she be cold? Then the thought hit her, settling into her skull like she'd been dunked in an icy pond. She took her mother's hand and it too was cold. She gently shook her, beseeching her to wake up. She shook her harder and harder and finally fell to her knees sobbing hysterically. Her mother -- the lone friend, enemy, bane and gift she had in the world was dead.

Hearing her cries, the chambermaids came running into the room. They couldn't comfort the beautiful young woman; they had no words, no gestures that could offer her anything. So, she cried and cried. Her father was away, of course, as he always was, at a meeting with some important and influential town member. Never had she seen her father move so quickly as he tore into the quiet room. He ran to his wife's side and clutched her, shaking, heaving and sobbing in loud and heartbreaking lamentations. Farayne stood and moved away from her mother, allowing her father time with his one and only love. But she caught it…she caught the look in his eyes as he looked at her, no matter how brief. It was as if he were saying, 'you caused your mother to be ill and now you have caused her death. Damn you.'

Farayne looked again and her father was holding her mother, his old, but still handsome face buried in her hair. Had she imagined the look? She glanced at the maids and they were looking at her, then quickly darted their eyes away. No, the look had been genuine, the emotion behind it one of pure fury and everyone saw it. Then as if he forgot himself, her father released her mother, stood and clasped his only child to him, hugging his beautiful daughter tightly. It was as if now that her mother was gone, he had to focus his energies somewhere -- his daughter -- and he had *total* control over her now. He no longer had to divide his domineering power over two women, one of them who fought him at least a little…his wife. There would no longer be any interference from his wife…nothing to stop him. His daughter would be his to mold and he would make her into what he wanted her to be.

"It is only you and I now my sweet Farayne. Your mother has gone where nothing can hurt her any longer. She will always be young, beautiful and healthy. She has not one care left and certainly nothing that should make us despair."

The words were kind but Farayne could not believe the emotion behind them. Far too much had passed between she and her father to think that it was all forgotten upon the death of the one painful thing they had in common.

FALLEN   VAN SCOYOC

Farayne looked up. In the distance, she could see the lights of Stoningham Green, her home -- her prison. She slowed her pace. Had she really been walking that fast? The estate of Anders Bowden was at least five miles from her home and the terrain that night bad at best. She was not in any hurry to get home, so why had she rushed? Could it have been the torrent of emotions that pushed her to move?

She breathed in a huge gulp of air and exhaled heavily. *Slow…yes, that's it…slow.*

The day of her mother's funeral seemed so surreal, so unemotional as if she were watching it happen to someone else. Her mother had always been there for her, good or bad, she'd always been there. That sounded odd, but it was true. She'd never known life without her mother and now she was alone with a father who would make her existence unbearable — more so than he already had over the years. Maybe her mother had been lucky in being able to leave. It always seemed that it was the ones who died that caught the lucky breaks in life. It had always been that way it seemed to her, that the living were the ones who had to worry, bemoan, fret, endure hardship, pain and the trials of life, while the dead simply went on to a better place, a place where nothing from the realm where they'd lived could touch them. Was that really the reward for life, death and a free spirit, a soul no longer bogged down by the stress of *living*? Living seemed so simple to some people, but was it really? There were worries, there were money problems, there were broken hearts, there were fights, there were moments of grief--the dead no longer had to worry about any of that. They were free, they'd experienced the ultimate release…the just reward for playing life's game and surviving every tribulation that fate could throw at them.

They deserved peace. They deserved that reward. Her mother deserved that peace…her mother deserved that reward. For putting up with her father for as long as she had, she deserved every crown, every golden brick under her foot in Heaven, every sparkling scepter…she'd *earned* it. Her father had never been a good husband to his beautiful wife. Had he known how to be? When a man was consumed with power, attaining it, getting more and keeping it was there room for anything else?

She looked at herself in the mirror and tied the black bow carefully. Her father insisted that she wear the ugliest dress in her closet for her mother's funeral. "To show respect," he'd said… "This is your mother's funeral, not a tea or a gala."

Farayne did not wish to attend her mother's funeral any more than she did a tea or a gala. Her father was not one to make her feel good about herself, at least not when he felt that he could glean more attention for *his* suffering.

She looked at herself one last time in the mirror and then stood. With a sigh, she turned quickly away from the reflective surface before she could catch sight of herself crying. Her father was waiting downstairs for her, to greet the guests. She would have to help out, to put on her best face and to be sociable; she knew that. It wasn't that she minded greeting their guests, at least not the ones that were genuine in their feelings and truly wished to pay their respects. But how many of them were there just for "show," just to make it known that they'd done the right thing, no matter how they actually felt about the Gleneden's? It was no secret that many in the town were envious of them, envious of both her parents, her father for the power he had over everyone it seemed, her mother for being beautiful while in the throes of a debilitating sickness and her, Farayne Gleneden, for being one of the most beautiful children ever born in the town.

FALLEN   VAN SCOYOC

She would know the ones who expressed genuine emotion.
It would be obvious to her. A wake was not the time to put on a
charade. She and her mother had done that enough in their lives
and now that time was passed. It was time for everyone to take off
the masks and show themselves for what they really were. But could
someone put on an act for so long and then leave that role
unscathed? Was there a time when actor and part became one and
the same...when a person could not tell fantasy from reality any
longer? So far she'd emerged unscathed from her many years of
make believe, but that was only because she had solace to take her
away from her role...someplace else that she could escape to rather
than this beauteous and divine life she pretended to live.

Farayne trudged down the stairs and caught sight of the
casket before her foot ever touched the bottom stair. She walked
slowly over to Analasiya Gleneden, her mother, her friend...the
woman who gave up the rest of her life to give her only child life.
She was laid out beautifully, surrounded by flowers and wearing a
dress specially made for her by the town's best seamstress.

The entire town gossiped about it after it happened. That
was how it was in her town, always had been, and always would be.
People were not happy unless they had something to whisper about.
The woman thought it a bit odd when the overwrought man
entered her shop asking her to measure his dead wife for a new
dress. But she knew the moment his dark head poked through the
door who he was. There would be no telling Danlyn Gleneden
"no," everyone knew that. So the babbling old bitches in town had
some new fodder to chew on until the next juicy slice of shameful
utterings came their way.

Farayne glared at the people who'd invaded her home and
taken away from her private time with her mother, a time when she
needed to be alone in her own world, grieving her own way. The
house was packed to capacity and for once, *she* was *not* the center of
attention. People were crying, people were talking, her mother's
real, *true* friends all looked pale and drawn while the hateful hags
who were just there for show were chatting, sipping tea as if at one
of their precious own affairs. As she walked through the crowd, she

received hugs from family and strangers alike. Those haughty women who normally would not have entertained even speaking to her without her mother present -- and then only did so out of propriety and deference to her standing in the community -- gave her hugs and "cheery" words of relief, but she felt nothing. Their words were hollow, spoken from dry and weathered old lips that lobbed harsh backstabbing cruelties behind any back that was unfortunate enough to be turned to them. They as people were meaningless to her and their sentiments were as flimsy as the milkweed that floated on the summer's breeze.

    Farayne walked over to her mother's casket and looked at her. She was still her mother, so lifelike, so real…so dead and yet so strangely alive for lack of a better description. Now that she thought about it, it fit the situation but she still loathed hearing people say, "They look just like they are sleeping!" Her mother wasn't sleeping…she was dead. Was this a cruel trick of death, to mock the living? Her mother's skin was still unwrinkled and though a little ashen she still looked the same. Was this a warning to the living that no matter how beautiful they were in life that once their lungs stopped breathing and their heart stopped beating that all that beauty would fade, disintegrate away like dust in a windstorm? Were the living really dying from the day they were born like some of her teachers claimed? Death was such an odd thing. How could someone still look the same once dead? How long would it take for her mother's skin to peel, to sag and then fall from the bones? How long before her beautiful dress crumbled with neglect? How long before her hair, with nothing to anchor it onto her head any longer would fall out or simply break away? Her thoughts were morbid, at least some would say that they were, but the cycle of life and death, the journey to the grave and then the possibilities afterward had always fascinated her -- although it was highly improper to speak of them. She touched her mother's cool cheek. Was she smiling? Her mother always loved a good party and as she got sicker that was one of the things she regretted the most, the inability to attend them. Farayne smiled through her years. She expected her mother to sit up at any moment and say "Farayne…what kind of party did you plan for me? Who is here? What teas did you pick and what delicacies did you have the cook prepare?"

Farayne smiled again then burst into tears. The small slivers of water ran down her cheek in tiny rivulets, dripping from her chin and onto the edge of the casket. She quickly wiped them away before someone would see.

She was gone...never to return to her except in dreams. There would be no waking up, there would be no more galas -- there would be no more anything. What would her life amount to now? Would her father take all of his anger and frustration out on her for a death that he surely blamed her for? She knew that he would control her more so now than ever, but would that control also be tempered with foul abuse? Or would he simply throw her to the streets, declaring that she'd been a curse on the family since her birth? *What* would happen to her?

Farayne wasn't sure how long she could stand there, how long she would stand there, but the world seemed to stop around her. Voices faded away, laughter disappeared and everything surrounding her became a blur of transition. She was in her own world and there she would stay, safe, hidden until summoned back to those that meant nothing to her.

Farayne was roused by the gentle hug. She didn't know why this hug made such a difference to her, to snatch her back into the land of the living, away from the realm of the nothing that she'd spent with her mother throughout the day, but it had. She looked at the person who'd hugged her. It was one of her chambermaids. Highly improper and certainly out of character for what was expected of a servant, Farayne didn't mind the familiarity with which she touched her.

"The Mistress looks so peaceful, my lady. I hope that she watches over all of us."

It was her favorite chambermaid and the one that she'd practically grown up with. There were ten of them in all, but this particular one...Temperance was her name, was her favorite. Only a few years older than Farayne, her mother was the head maid of the house. Like her mother had before her, Temperance had been groomed since the say of her birth to tend to her mother's and Farayne's needs. Never one to gossip or speak out of turn, she'd been a faithful hand around the Gleneden estate and Farayne truly liked her. She wondered if she'd ever taken the time to tell her just how much her service meant to her? Probably not. It was a shame to admit it and Farayne herself could not help but feel guilty for *thinking* it. It seemed that the only time anyone paid attention to their actions was when something as cold and hard a death slapped them in the face and forced them to see. In solemn shades and somber emotions, reality had a way of reminding people what they took for granted on a day-to-day basis.

Most of her maids were old or at least *older*. It was nice to have someone every once in a while close to her own age to talk to. Farayne made a mental note that she would be more appreciative of Temperance from that day forward.

"Thank you, Temperance. I know that my mother always liked you. You have been so good to us. I know I have never really said it, but thank you. Thank you for everything that you did for my mother and that you will continue to do for me."

The girl's lips trembled and then she smiled, curtsied quickly, bowing her blonde head in acquiescence and then darted away, her hands to her face.

Farayne smiled ruefully. Maybe her mother's funeral hadn't been the best time to express her gratitude, judging by the maid's reaction, but at least she felt better. That was one burden relieved from her shoulders. She had many, many more to go...

The day passed into the evening and the maids brought out plate after plate, platter after platter and serving after serving of food. Why were all these people still at her house? They'd viewed her mother's body, said their goodbyes and paid their respects. Yet, there they all were still in her parlor! Farayne once again retreated into her own little world, the calm and quiet place where she could be alone with her thoughts. She knew people had spoken to her, hugged her, caressed her and given her flowers and trinkets, but she'd paid no attention to any of them. The only thing that had brought her out of her world once again but the clatter of an empty and expensive plate as it fell to the floor. Farayne's head snapped up. That was when she noticed just how full the parlor still was and her nose tempted by the delicious smells that saturated the room. She got up and looked around. Gone were the tears, gone were the exclamations of loss...her father had turned her mother's funeral into a lavish dinner party! He was smoking, he was smiling and he was chatting with his friends and associates. Her mother's true friends had all left, as was proper for a wake for a loved one or dear friend, and all that was left of the supposed *grievers* were the arrogant bitties who could not care less about anyone within the walls of the Gleneden estate!

Farayne had been exposed to enough parties to know that using people was all part of the game. She knew the routine as well as he father did she'd watched him enough times, despising him increasingly with each story he told and each hand he shook. It would start with a fancy and very confident introduction. Then once the door was opened and the contact made it would escalate to a promise of something that only her father could give them -- in exchange for something he needed. Bribe them a little if necessary, then deliver, establish the foundation as a man that could get the impossible or at the least the inconvenient done. The accumulation of power would be eminent and once that power was established, deep-rooted power, it would take an act of immense proportions (or someone with greater power) to upseat the person with the most influence.

Her father had played the game a long time and he was the best at it as far as she was concerned, but *this was her mother's wake for God's sake*! His wife's dead body lay in the same room and as if she were someone else's wife, he'd forgotten that she'd died. This was not a happy affair! This was *not* the time to be making new alliances and gaining more power. This was his wife, the mother of his child, the woman he'd bedded as a pure white virgin, loved and sworn to love until death did them part. Death had done them part and he'd already moved on to other 'business' it seemed! How could he? *How dare he?*

It was then that she realized that within the walls of Stoningham Green she would stay trapped unless she simply left her father's clutches. He would be the devoted widower, raising an almost adult daughter on his own. He would be pitied, he would be lauded and he would be elevated to sainthood. The power that he would gain from such deeds would be the envy, even more so, of the entire town and he would revel in it. Farayne was so angry that she could scarcely see. She stomped up the stairs and to her room. Throwing herself on her bed, she sobbed her heart out. That was the night that she would never forget. No matter how long she lived she would never forget how not even in death her mother could be remembered for the caring and giving wife, mother and member of the community shed always been. No matter how ill, if her mother could help out in some way in the town, she did. She would sew, she would knit, she did whatever her body would allow her to in order to help those that needed it and how had she been repaid? By having her wake turned into a spectacle, a business deal and an extravaganza by her father, looking to capitalize on his *sacrifice.*

The tears burned her face badly as she cried. She didn't remember going to sleep that night.

She stopped again. She was almost home. She wiped her eyes and face. She'd been crying and hadn't even realized it. She might as well finish her painful trek through the last day that she would ever physically see her mother. She still had a little way to go, home was not going anywhere and she certainly was in no hurry to

get there. With a sigh she did the same thing she'd done all night --
put one foot in front of the other and allow her mind to wander.

The day was so hot, so stifling hot but Farayne hardly felt
any thing. Her mother was leaving. She was going away never to
return. She knew she'd had the same feelings at her wake, but that
had been so surreal. Her mother was right there, right in front of
her. She could still see her, she could still touch her…she wasn't
dead to her, not in memory, not in body, not in spirit…not yet. She
would never forget her mother of course, but the reality of her loss
would not manifest itself until her mother was physically gone from
her sight. She knew that and it was so difficult for her to bear.

The scenario was all too familiar to her. She once again sat
in front of her vanity, tying back her beautiful hair and smoothing
her second ugliest dress in her wardrobe. Of course her father was
making her wear yet another article of clothing that she wished
she'd never owned, *out of respect*. That word struck her as so odd and
she had to stifle a giggle. If it wouldn't take so much strength to do
so, she would have outright laughed. *Respect*. What did *he* know of
respect? He had none for anyone, including her mother. He could
throw a gala party at his wife's wake, entertain people in his home
whom had despised her and that was all right. Yet she wished to
wear something pretty to her mother's final day on earth and she
could not because it would be disrespectful to draw any attention to
herself, away from her mother. Farayne picked up her hairbrush
and threw it across the room. The glass handle shattered. Not that
she cared.

Déjà vu…déjà vu…she shook her head, fighting back the
tears she already felt welling in her swollen eyes. Would the same
thing happen at her mother's funeral as had at her wake? Oh no, it

would have to be something grander than simple business alliances. Would her father announce a new woman in his life, someone to help him run the homestead? Would she be someone with immense wealth, connections, property, and multiple businesses, someone that he could use that money to attain an ungodly amount of influence until he couldn't be stopped?

As much as she missed her mother already, she wanted the day to be over with. It was so unfair what her father was doing. Her mother deserved a send off to the beyond fitting for a queen…not to be used as a tool to gain money, fame and prominence -- which the family and particularly her father, already had.

It had been only two days since her mother's wake and her father wasn't wasting any time in disposing of his wife of twenty years. He claimed that she would have wanted it that way, for them to continue on with their lives, not dwelling on her unfortunate passing. Farayne pursed her lips. Maybe she was being too hard on her father. Maybe he simply could not cope with his love's death and therefore did anything, no matter how poor in taste to take his mind off the fact that when he woke in the morning, his first thoughts would be only a memory of her. No matter his desire to see her, she would not miraculously appear to him as she had when she was younger. As a child, Farayne had never understood her parent's desire for separate bedrooms, but as she got older that lonely room had been her mother's escape from a man that surely she'd grown away from. How could her mother have loved someone like her father? Farayne hadn't paid a lot of attention to familial business as she was growing up, at least not to her father's mannerisms. Had he always been so dictatorial or had that only happened after he could not control the one thing in his life that he wished he could…his wife's health? It was no secret that her father controlled everything -- and everyone. He always had. But there were some things that not even the great Danlyn Gleneden could control, things that were beyond his scope of power and that influence, money and fame had no sway over.

She wished that she could simply walk up to him and say, "Father…when did you become such a bastard? Was it when I maimed mother during my birth, or was it when it sunk in that I was not only not a male child but that you had no other chance to sire one?"

As much as she would relish being able to do so, she knew that she could not.

She almost didn't hear the faint knock at the door. The maid, eyes down, stuck her head in just enough to be seen. Farayne had half hoped that it would be Temperance.

"My lady Farayne, your father wishes you to come down now. It is time to lay your mother to eternal rest."

Just as quickly as the woman was there, she just as quickly was gone. Farayne sighed heavily and stood. Yes, déjà vu all over again. She walked out of her room, slamming the door as hard as she could. If anyone asked...it was the wind, it took the door away from her. They wouldn't question...

Farayne stepped off the stairs as she had for her mother's wake and walked up to her father, eyes downcast, much the same as the maid had done and simply stood. She didn't wish to speak to him, she certainly didn't wish to look at him, she merely wanted to go, bury her mother and return to her own little world, the only place where she could truly be comfortable.

Her father looked at her, she could feel his eyes boring into her. She could always feel it when he looked at her.

"Are you ready to go my dear daughter, my one and only and most precious angel, the light of my life?"

Farayne had to physically fight throwing up. Her father did not have to bribe her with words as he did his business associates. He did not have to play to her ego and offer empty flattery to her to make her love him. She did, she loved him deeply although she did not like him and she certainly had no respect for him.

She nodded her answer and with his hand gently guiding her, they walked outside to the awaiting carriage.

The trip to the church and cemetery was silent. She had nothing to say and neither did he, which suited Farayne just fine. She couldn't help but silently wonder if her father felt even the smallest bit of guilt over his actions at her mother's wake and maybe that was why, when faced with a church, priest and the need for atonement he was suddenly meek. It would serve him right…

The carriage stopped, she got out and in a trance-like state followed her father to the awaiting large and beautiful cemetery. Only the richest were buried in the *Eternal Passage* cemetery, so of course her mother would have to be interred amongst only the finest ever-lasting companions. Farayne had always loved the graves, crypts and statues that made up the churchyard. Statues of angels, cherubs, horses and carriages, trees, books and crypts bigger than most stables caught her eyes. Her mother would surely have one of the finest crypts to be seen in all of town, she was certain of it. However, she would be wrong…she simply did not know just how wrong. What should have been a grand and respectful tribute to her mother was a gaudy display and tawdry show of money, Farayne stopped, nearly bumping into her father as he stopped so suddenly. She lifted her head and saw the large, iron gates of the cemetery before them. Winding morning glories played their part in welcoming visitors. Farayne had always loved morning glories but this day they did not give her the comfort they had in the past. On this day there would be no comfort. She ventured ahead of her father and into the cemetery, scarcely hearing him.

"My dear…what do you think? This plot, right here in the front, in the biggest piece of land left in the cemetery is the gravesite of your mother. I wanted her eternal home to be something that she would forever treasure as she looks down on us visiting her, and watches over us at the estate."

Farayne's eyes opened widely, and she burst into tears.

"Yes my sweet. This tribute to a woman such as your mother elicits such emotion from me as well."

Farayne was speechless. She was so angry that her skin literally burned. How dare her father turn her mother's burial site into a marble museum! The only thing "real" about the gravesite was the ancient oaks that seemed to stand sentry over the spot. The closest grave was at least two hundred yards away. This particular spot had never been purchased for graves before because *no one* had been able to afford to do so! The land was supposedly donated to the church for some form of memory garden for the deceased within the cemetery walls. That was the last Farayne heard of it.

32

"But father, I thought this land was donated to the church?"

She hated the smug expression on her father's face as he answered.

"It *had* been my dear, but not just *any* place would be good enough for your mother! I gave the church a tidy sum for this spot. Is it not wonderful?"

Farayne cried harder. Of course, it would be her father to flaunt their wealth once again and do what no one else in town had been able to do!

Even Farayne's eyes burned as she looked at her mother's final resting place. The entire area was squared off and surrounded by a low, decorative brick and mortar wall with freshly planted peach colored rose bushes adorning every few feet. She ventured though the only open spot, which she could only imagine served as an invisible gate of sorts and into the plot. A bench sat directly in front of the gravestone and was inscribed in beautifully elegant lettering, "In loving memory." Farayne continued to take in everything around her, her skull on fire and her eyes feeling as if they would explode from her head. The headstone at the base of her mother's grave was fine, it was the rest of the "display" that infuriated her. The base was large, at least five feet tall, square, solid marble, imported at the greatest expense she was certain, covered with her mother's favorite epitaph…"Her spirit stands on that bright shore and softly whispers weep no more," the epitaph that she'd told both husband and daughter many years before that she'd want were she to die first. But as Farayne's eyes traveled up, she could not believe what she saw. On top of the base of the gravestone was a large ball, roughly three feet high. It was simple, just a large, round, ball-shaped piece of marble. On top of that was a flat, large piece of marble that looked like a tabletop. On top of the tabletop was an intricate carving of a horse, complete with bridle and saddle. Sitting in the saddle was her mother, sitting side saddle of course like a lady should, hair coiffed perfectly, crisp riding outfit, her hat tilted at such an elegant angle and a smile creasing her perfect lips.

"Your mother was always such an accomplished rider. I wanted her to ride into eternity in the grandest of style."

Farayne didn't think her father meant the words as an insult. After all this was her mother's funeral and even though he'd shown what little true class he had, it would be intolerable and downright unforgivable to make rude and slighting comments to his daughter as she buried her mother. However, Farayne took them as the barbs she felt them to be.

Farayne knew that before she ruined her body, her mother had been quite a rider. She used to take her horse out often and ride it, according to what she told her. That was part of the reason why, when her daughter turned twelve, she insisted on expensive lessons for her to learn how to ride, so she could follow in her mother's footsteps and ride with the ease of the greatest equestrians. But Farayne had never been interested. She liked horses and she could ride, but what did being able to do so allow her? Nothing. Being able to ride a horse was a necessary part of life for men, but what purpose did it serve for a woman? Maybe one day it would for her…

She continued to look at the tasteless gravestone that would mark her mother's final resting place. In one corner stood a perfect -- in size, dimension and detail -- statue of Farayne and in the opposite corner stood one of her father. The Farayne statue chilled the young woman. It was as if she were attending *her own* funeral and not her mother's. The statue was garbed in a long, flowing dress with frills at the three quarter inch sleeves, frills at the neck, and gloves on her tiny hands one of which held a parasol. She hated… absolutely *loathed and despised* those things but her father insisted that she carry one, and a beautiful hat with lace and flowers titled at the perfect angle on her head. Her long hair was tucked up inside the hat, her eyes seemed to smile and a kind expression decorated her perfect face. It made her sick. Her father had also taken the opportunity to make certain that he would be immortalized in as perfect of fashion as he could as well. He was attired in a stately jacket, knee length of course as most men of his prominence wore, long, frilled sleeves, fancy buttons on the coat, a decorative ascot, shiny boots, as shiny as they could look being carved out of marble, one hand reaching up to his wife and the other resting at his side. His hair was perfect, his face smooth and he was so very handsome. Farayne knew that if he desired another wife, one that could possibly give him the boy child he so desperately wanted that he would have no trouble procuring a new mate.

"Lovely isn't my dear? I think I did quite a wonderful job in immortalizing us all."

Farayne nodded…that was all she could do.

The funeral was about to start and it was then that Farayne noticed them…the carriages. Ornate and elegant carriages were lined up for what seemed like miles though Farayne knew that was an exaggeration. Women wept, men kept their heads low. She fumed. Ashamed, all of them, *they should feel so shameful* for turning her mother's wake into an extravaganza and then trying to atone by seeming melancholy and solemn, something that would have suited for the wake, at her mother's burial.

She scarcely remembered anything else that happened that day. The priest's words were just that, words. They gave her no comfort, they meant as little to her as the 'condolences' she'd received at her mother's wake. No one knew for certain what was going to happen to her mother's body, no one knew for certain that her soul would live on, that she was no longer suffering in a body that was useless to her. She believed in an afterlife and she believed that people got what they deserved after they died, but who was to judge *what* they got?

It was that day, during the service, after her father's brazen display of inconsideration as to how her mother's memory would be preserved for eternity that she decided that she would no longer feel for her father the way she had. She would love him because he was her father just as she always had, but she didn't respect him and she would simply exist within the dwelling they called "home." She would share nothing with him that was not absolutely vital to her existence, she would make no memories of him as she had with her mother, she would simply dwell within the walls of the estate and continue her treks into her woods, sharing moments alone and with the solitude that she gleaned from those moments. She would not fight with him; she would not allow him to anger her, to make her feel guilt over anything nor to dominate her any more than he already did.

Until such time came as she could escape, she had to have a place to stay, she had to have food, she had to have clothing and she would do what was necessary to survive. Her father seemed to know when to leave her alone, he seemed to know when she'd had enough so she would take those moments of victory and hold them to her, using them to hearten her as she plotted a way to escape. Her mother held on, for so many years she'd held on and survived. She would as well...

Farayne looked up and she was there...at the gates of her estate. Gone was the heartbreaking memory of her mother's horrendous send off, gone was the intense wrath she'd felt at the time for her father...that wrath and near hatred had diminished to a slow and simmering boil, a boil that she could tolerate and had learned quite well to since her mother's passing. Gone were the people she despised, feigning sadness at the funeral. The moon illuminated her path the wind had picked up and seemed to push her along as if nudging her closer to home. She took the last few steps to the front of the entrance and stopped. She looked through the beckoning iron poles flanked with bright red, winding roses and felt so alone. She *was* alone. From the outside, this was a castle, an abode that commanded respect and awe from allies, friends and strangers alike. This was the home that all her peers secretly wished they lived in. This was *her* home and yet it was as foreign to her as the gala she'd just escaped from. Home had to be where one was happy, where one could cultivate good memories, that was what her mother had always said. If that were true, then she'd never had a home. Never. She'd never been happy in her father's house, *she'd never been.*

FALLEN   VAN SCOYOC

She pushed open the gate, and then closed it behind her. With a sigh born of weariness, she trudged to the home that was simply a roof over her head.

She knew it would happen and she was prepared for it. Her father would be furious beyond reckoning that she left the party early. She was his trophy to show off as if to say, "Look what a fine job I have done in raising my daughter all alone. No man could have done as great a job as I have with no wife at his side!" She would counter his anger smoothly and with the grace of the noblewoman she was, if it came to that. His screaming, as he often did now that she had learned how to fight a battle of not only wills, but of wits to boot. He didn't like having his own tactics used against him, the beguiling charms that he so quickly used on others, she too had learned. It was a different story all together when she used those same treatments on him. She already knew what she was going to say when he demanded to know why she'd left him embarrassed and stranded.

She would tell him the truth. In as puny and pathetic a voice as she could muster she would tell him that she was heartsick. That since her sweet Temperance left the estate for marriage, that she'd been so sad. He hadn't forgotten that she'd grown up with Temperance had he? She felt more as if she'd lost a sister than a maid.

She was certain that such a story would silence him. It had to. What could he say to that? It was true to a degree and as long as there was a grain of truth to it, she could be convincing.

As sure as if it had been planned, when Danlyn Gleneden came storming into the house later that night thundering at her about her leaving him humiliated at the party, she put on her best act and it worked. She was irate at his presumptions, and his audacity infuriated her further. He stank of cigar smoke, he reeked of alcohol and he had a winning smile on his face as if he'd sealed the deal of a lifetime with someone, even as he yelled at her.

"I give you my humblest apologies father, but I have been so heartsick since Temperance left. You do know that she and I grew up together? Oh father, please don't tell me that you forgot that! She was more like a friend than a maid...and I felt as if she were *the sister I never had*. I miss her so much. It was not that I was in a hurry to get back here this night, knowing that she would not be here, but seeing so many of those girls, sweet, wispy...they all reminded me of my dear Temperance."

She sobbed as pathetically as her story made her out to be. She'd been correct...her father could say nothing, save for stammering an apology. With a swift kiss to her raven head, he disappeared to his room. She did not see or hear from him for the remainder of the night and that was just how she wished it to be.

The wind caressed her face, the sun bathed her in the warmest light, she could hear the sheep in the distance as they bleated and the birds sang sweetly to her. She still savored her victory from the pervious evening. She had all but laughed in her sleep as she etched the expression from her father's face into her mind. The trip this morning outside had been especially sweet in remembrance of that great evening and she had relished every beam of sunlight that tickled her, every blade of grass she passed and each cloud in the sky. How she wished sometimes that she could live outside! It was much more peaceful and much more comforting to her than the stuffy old stone walls of her room. Her curtains were always open, allowing the sunshine in, the windows were open when the weather was nice and many times she sat on the plush chair in the sunlight and read.

But no matter how much she tried to make her room a light and airy dream escape, she simply couldn't. One glance over her shoulder, one look around her room, though beautiful, reminded her that she was a prisoner.

Farayne kicked the ground in disgust as she walked the perfectly manicured lawn of her estate. There had to be more to life...there simply *had* to be. She had been troubled since that night at the party. That night was *it* for her -- she had been pushed to the breaking point. Every waking minute since that night had been spent plotting a way to escape her boring life and start someplace new. But she had no knowledge, not any that would help her survive outside the estate. She couldn't cook, she had no idea how to grow things to eat...she wouldn't last two days and she knew it. Education seemed increasingly inviting to her, an education that would serve her well enough to free her from the stifling clutches of court life. If she could educate herself on more than fine arts, music and etiquette, maybe she wouldn't become like those that begged at her home for food and water. She could not help but think of how many of them had been like her at one time. How many of them had entertained the same thoughts she did day and night? How many of them had finally found freedom, only to starve or have to beg and steal to survive?

She shook her head. She knew there were people who lived off the land, those who were always dirty but content. She wished to know about them and she wished to delve into the arcane knowledge that everyone deemed so evil. Could she find someone to trade educations with her? She'd be more than happy to give anyone a classical education in exchange for an informal, but actually useful, education in life itself and how to survive. Farming and growing things was more important than writing if one lived off the land, but it did not hurt to know how to write one's name. An education might help someone of less breeding get more money for their wares at the market or net them some form of privilege that they might not otherwise get if they were deemed stupid or simple. But how could she educate herself without the constraints of being watched, her schedule being dictated to her, and most importantly, without her father's disapproval? No matter what she did his eyes was always on her and the servant girls feared him immensely so they dared not to do everything he said.

Farayne kicked the ground again and looked up. A shepherd was watching her. *See, I cannot do one thing without being watched, by someone!*

She began to trudge back to the house, her mind still furiously muddled and her head pounding from thinking so hard. Then, as if the clouds of her mind were being blown away by Zephyr himself, a thought struck her.

She was the curious sort and always had been. She thought back to the times she had gone on adventures to places that she was never supposed to set foot upon. Of course, they were all on the estate and right within her own home to be exact, but they were still forbidden. Had it not been for her overt curiosity and her determined thinking of how to escape for her biggest adventure of all, she might have never found the means with which to do her research. However, her brain had cooperated, fate had smiled on her and she knew what she could do, although the thought occurred to her completely by accident. *Was this fate?* Or was she simply too stubborn to *not* get her way?

Farayne smiled as if a child holding onto a secret that others would be anxious to hear. In a way she was. Though many would think her mad if they could see into her mind, didn't they, to a degree, already? Most other women she knew would do anything in order to catch the eye of a handsome, young man like Ronan Tanserlyn. Yet, he vied for her company and she wished nothing to do with him. She wished for nothing to do with him or any man like him. She was not a prize to be had, a brooch to be pinned upon one's breast to show off to the world one's status. She was a woman, a lady, a child, a wife…a mother – or at least she would be one day and it would be with the man of *her* choosing!

Farayne smiled as she crept quietly down the stairs, past the scullery maids singing, napping and bickering in the kitchen, out the door, willing it with all her might not to squeak. She closed the door behind her and giggled softly.

She all but ran to the stables lest some prying maid see her, praying that the horses would not be startled at her approach and let anyone know she was there, and out the back gate where no one would ever think to look for her. No one cared about the stables and the stable hands weren't thought of any more than the horses themselves were, so what would they care what she did? The horses on the other hand made noise at any approach, sound or ripple in their horse world. She willed them not to give her away this night.

She was gleeful in her wickedness. This would be her first night *alone* outside of Stoningham and she was ready for an adventure – a real adventure. She just hoped that no one would come check on her too closely and notice that the pillows under the covers were not her.

At first she felt somewhat guilty about sneaking away, but the more she walked, the more she knew that she was doing the right thing for herself. The deplorable attitudes of her peers and even the older class of attendees at the last gala *she ever planned to attend* had shown her all she needed to know about the life that she had been born into. She had never fit in, finding out at a very early age that they were not the sort of people that she wished to convene with, not with *any* of them and she wished nothing to do with their haughty ways.

How she wished for someone different to talk to, someone she actually had something in common with. How she wished to know of the lives of others and what it was like to live as they did. How she wished to know of farm life and hard times instead of having everything handed to her. How would she ever learn the importance of anything if she had everything given to her? She sighed because she knew that finding a down-to-earth person from her own class with which to share *any* of her hopes and dreams would be impossible.

It was not chilly this night and she had chosen her "worst" to go out in. Her hair was down, reaching almost to her waist, instead of tied up in the fancy coifs her chambermaid insisted she wear. She smiled as she thought back to how she had collected her ensemble.

She felt like a ghost as the writhed her way around walls and hid from the house staff as she set her sights on the goal – the attic stairs. It was late and everyone was asleep except the kitchen staff. It was just her luck that the steps, the *only* steps, to the attic would be at the back of the kitchen. She prayed that they wouldn't see her. They normally didn't pay a lot of attention to anything anyway, except the expensive cooking wines they conned her father into buying for them, which they drank instead of cooked with. They kept unusual hours -- up at dawn and in bed in the wee hours. No wonder there had to be so many of them, so they could work in shifts!

Her father would be furious if he knew that she wished to go up to the attic. The attic was on the fifth floor and some place that was never discussed. Oh it was whispered about by the staff and mostly by the maids who never passed up the opportunity to gossip, but to actually refer to the *attic* in conversation was all but forbidden. She stifled her giddiness and climbed the stairs as quickly but as quietly as possible.

She stood looking at the door, her heart in her throat. Her hands shook as she reached for the knob. It didn't feel like her own hand as she turned the cold knob and then ran into the room, closing the door behind her and leaning heavily against it. As her eyes adjusted to the darkness, she held her breath. Would anyone venture up those spooky stairs after her? It was so early in the morning, was anyone but the stable boys and kitchen staff awake?

She smiled as she rested her head against the hard door. She had always loved the attic, though her father's wrath would be unholy were he to catch her there. "A lady should not be traipsing about in a dust laden old room with nothing but hollow and useless memories of times gone by," he had bellowed to her in times past when she expressed an interest in visiting the forgotten room.

FALLEN   VAN SCOYOC

She did not know why her father was so against her visiting the attic, but it did not matter. She had a plan and just knew that what she would need to implement that plan lie in that old and decayed part of the house.

She allowed her eyes to relax and suddenly she could see a little better. One small, stained and oddly shaped window threw light into the chilly realm, showing her what adventure awaited her.

There was an old dress hanging on a rack. It was moldy and torn but looked to be very fancy. Was it a wedding gown?

Farayne stepped away from the door, willing herself to leave the safety she felt there. She haltingly approached the dress and reached out to it. Her hands grasped fragile and paper-like material that crumbled to the touch. The dress appeared to be a wedding gown. Was it her mother's gown maybe? Farayne did not want to think about why the dress had been relegated the unused room. She surmised that it brought back painful memories for her father so he didn't wish to see it again.

As she stood in the pale sunlight that trickled into the room, she smiled and silently clapped her hands like a child who had been presented with a surprise. For a while, she simply wandered around the cobweb-infested kingdom, taking in all the treasures that had long since been forgotten.

Cloths covered much of the attic's contents but one thing did catch her eye. As if calling out to her and luring her with a tantalizing treasure that she could not pass up, an ancient trunk sat against the far wall right under the odd window.

She almost squealed with joy as she scurried across the dusty floor and to her knees in front of it. She ran her hands across the cobwebbed coffer and gently lifted the lid. The box had been abused badly it seemed. Locks that were meant to keep the curious out, were gone, ripped out or smashed away. She slapped her hands to her mouth as a cloud of choking dust and trunk particles assailed her. She tried her hardest to stifle a cough but it escaped her throat, tearing into the quiet room like a thousand armies bent on destruction. She clamped her hand over her mouth again and forced the cough into her chest, her body contorting in spasms as she fought the need for her lungs to expel their violators.

She waved her hand, not that it did a lot of good, to clear her vision as the angry mass coated her eyes as well, but she succeeded in eventually clearing the air somewhat to see very old, worn out clothing. She stifled another cough, wiped her eyes on her skirt and reached eagerly into the trunk.

Her hands pulled out a large item of clothing that too seemed to protest being disturbed, by sending another attack of dust against her. She stood and held the item out to see it fully. It was a dress -- simple and mouse-eaten but it would serve her well. The people she wished to learn from did not dress like royalty and neither should she to meet them.

She knelt again at the trunk and pulled another article out. It had been white at one time but was yellowed with age and neglect. The once glorious petticoat was tattered but who would see it under her dress? She reached one last time into the trunk. The last offering from the lonely chest was an even poorer blouse and a length of faded ribbon. She really had no examples of impoverished clothing on which to base her ensemble, but did it really matter since she was supposed to be poor? She had seen some of the beggar women with long blouses worn over their dresses and tied at the waist with flimsy belts. She would simply substitute the ribbon for a belt. It was probably supposed to be for her glorious crowning of ebon hair but that would also have to look like that of a poor person. She had to blend in with those that she wished to study and learn from! She didn't know exactly whom it was that she supposed to find, this dream collection of people to satisfy her curiosity, but she figured if she walked long enough she would find someone that was dressed in the manner she was.

Farayne quickly removed her simple skirt and donned the sad clothing. She had spied a once breathtaking oval mirror in a corner, half covered, when she first got into the attic. She remembered that mirror from her childhood and had always loved it. She wondered many times over the years what had happened to it. She quietly ran to it, jerking the cloth away to see herself as others would. The ancient mirror that had once belonged to her great, great grandmother showed her a stunning beauty in hideous clothing. Nothing could detract from her beauty it seemed. Maybe she could smear dirt on her face and arms? No, she couldn't do that, as her chambermaid would have a fit if she saw her dirty and then she would fuss even more over her. Farayne stomped her foot in anger then immediately cringed. Her heart seemed to stop and her foot felt glued to the floor. That would be all she would need, for the butler to come rushing up the stairs to investigate the source of the racket and find her there. She held her breath and no one came. Luckily for her, most of the staff thought the attic to be haunted and would not step foot near it. Ghosts or no ghosts, the attic held the key to the life she wished to know about and so the transparent inhabitants would simply have to tolerate her presence. Farayne went back to admiring herself in the mirror. She did look quite a bit like the beggars that had come so many times to her home. She saw an old and decaying cape hanging on a hook on the wall and she pulled it down. It was threadbare and worn in many places. A thin piece of rope through the hood would serve as the tie to shield her face from prying eyes. She was very proud of herself.

She stifled a loud giggle as she once again thought of how furious her father would be if he knew that she had blatantly disobeyed him by going to the attic. It didn't matter. Sneaking, unbeknownst to anyone, up those stairs had given her a thrill that she could not readily explain. The prospect of going out, alone, in the black of night made her heart pound with excitement – something she worried that she would never feel.

Her breath seemed to cling to her throat as she caught sight of her destination, barely visible in the thick night fog that enveloped the air. She knew she was going to someplace forbidden, someplace a lady of her social standing didn't dare go. *But she was going…*

She was excited to be part of another life, even if only for a while. She continued to stand at the edge of town. It was deserted except for a light in the distance. Most of the lanterns had burned out, but the moon helped light her path and, as she had in the attic, if she allowed her eyes to adjust, she could see well enough to make her way. But her feet for some reason would not move. She wished them to, but it was as if something was holding her back…something that knew better than she that she should not be there. Nothing would stop her though. *Nothing.*

The shops were closed and the fog, while beautiful, blanketed everything in a quiet gloom. Farayne stopped to appreciate the solitude for just a moment. Many times, she would get up before the rising of the sun and simply stare out her window. It was in that pre-dawn passage of time, before the world awoke, that she felt the most at peace. Nothing made her happier than to watch the rising of the sun. There was something about watching the black of night fade to the pale orange of the morn that she simply could not describe.

She looked again at her final destination. The town really was peaceful although this section of town was desolate. Maybe that was when one could see a town for what it really was, when no one was about making it look lively with business, merriment and day-to-day happenings. No one of her breeding would dare come to the Rynd District even during the day, let alone in the middle of the night. It was an area of taverns and brothels where thugs, dregs and women of ill repute carried on their despicable ways. Murders were as common in this area as teatime was in her world.

She looked up and found that she was closer now to her goal. Her feet had moved, though she didn't remember them doing so. She was closer to the light and could just make out the sign as it hid behind a thick haze, almost as if willing her not to see it for what it was. It was a pub, the Dancing Dragon Pub. People were walking in and out, music was playing, and it was loud. This would be perfect. She pulled her hood tighter around her milky white face and moved forward.

FALLEN   VAN SCOYOC

The tavern was loud, very loud after her commune with such a quiet evening and she found herself assailed by many sights and smells, most of them horribly unpleasant, as she stepped inside. She almost turned around and went back home but she couldn't. She would go inside and she would have her night of adventure. Even if she decided never to come back, at least she had partly done what she set out to do…see how those of lesser ilk than herself lived.

Farayne trembled with terrified excitement as she looked around in awe at her surroundings. If she hadn't been so curious as to the goings on, she would indeed have fled as fast as she could back to the safety of her home. She hurried further into the pub to a table in the back. She would remain quiet this night; she would draw no attention to herself although it was clear that she had caught the eye of every scoundrel in the room as she walked in. She would watch and she would wait. Knowledge and fulfillment would be hers she simply needed to be patient.

CHAPTER TWO
LIFE AT THE DANCING DRAGON

Farayne hurried to her table in the back of the room. She was grateful that each time she went to *her* table, it was always empty. Many times, she wondered if the table being empty was intentional, so that she could be watched and set upon if the opportunity presented itself or if the table was always empty because it was the furthest away from the merriment everyone enjoyed. She didn't know what she would do if she ever walked in and saw someone else occupying the hidden alcove. Every night for the past month, she'd been going to the Dancing Dragon Pub and each night she learned something new, or at least something that was new to her.

Crude words, strange customs, odd mannerisms, unintelligent speech, lewd suggestions, superstitions…she had seen it all in just a month's time and though some of it deeply offended her -- made her sick to think of what the vagabonds meant -- and scared her, she was still just as fascinated as she had been that first night. She had even tried begging for money to buy the rough ale that the people drank. Most of the time, she was refused and one night a woman who thought Farayne was competing for her 'business' threw her out onto the street. Bruised and sore she had trudged the long trip home, but returned the next night. Once again, the tacky trollop assailed her and threw her out onto the street.

Digging deep into her own heart for all the horrible things she had seen her fellow class do to people and what she had learned courtesy of the people at the pub, Farayne let loose a torrent of vile filth that left the woman speechless. In closing, her words were a bit more eloquent, but not as much as she was accustomed to them being.

"You fat, grotesque pig, if I wanted your business, do you not think I could have it at *any time* I wished? You should be *thanking* me and giving me a pittance of what you make in grateful appreciation that I haven't taken any food from your table, although it would not hurt you to lose a few pounds! I am *gorgeous* while you are an abomination! Look at you," which everyone instinctively did, much to Farayne's delight, "the very thought of a man *willingly* sharing his bed with *you* is repulsive! *You* should be paying *them* for exposing them to your hideousness!"

The tavern-goers stood in shock at the tiny girl's outburst. The woman, drunk as she was, took a swing at Farayne who quickly dodged her attack. That was something else that Farayne had learned while at the pub…self defense. She always watched the numerous fights (which broke out each night) and decided to employ a bit of what she'd learned. She kicked the woman in her rear-end so hard that she landed on a table and broke it. The tavern owner came around the bar in a fury and jerked the woman up by her greasy, red hair, forcing her, right there in front of everyone, to hand over enough money to pay for the table. Farayne tossed her shiny black hair and went back to her table -- which was empty as usual -- and stayed unmolested the remainder of the night.

From that night forward, the tavern-goers looked at her differently and the prostitute gained a newfound respect for Ebony, as Farayne told people her name was. The tavern owner also paid for all of Farayne's drinks in appreciation for her standing up to the woman who was more trouble than she was worth. According to him, she ran off more business than she brought in, the table was not the first piece of furniture that she had broken, whether by falling on it in a drunken stupor or by using it in a fight and she picked fights with anyone who would not acquiesce to her advances.

The whore had a change of heart after her confrontation with such a small keg of brewing anger, and as much as she was capable of with no education or breeding, exchanged pleasantries with the razor-tongued girl every night as they passed each other.

In time, Farayne was considered a regular and she and Tansy the Trollop became fast friends. Ebony and Tansy always looked out for one another and any man who solicited her for things that she had no inclination to do she would direct them to Tansy who was only more than happy to oblige them.

If often bothered Farayne that some people were still suspicious of her. She knew that although the people that inhabited the tavern were ignorant -- in the literal sense — they were not all of them totally stupid. In the Rynd District a person was not stupid and alive very long unless they were exceptionally lucky. She knew that the day might come when people would question her story of how and why she spent her nights in such a lowly place as the Dancing Dragon, and she was ready for the doubters. Because the Rynd District was small and no one recognized her as living there she had crafted a carefully detailed story of how she found her way there. Though enigmatic about exactly *how* she found the pub and why she would want to go there, she seemed to have an answer for every question asked of her.

After a particularly aggravating grilling one evening by some of the patrons she decided that she'd endured enough.

"I was, am, a maid by trade as was my mother and my grandmother before me. I got kicked off the estate where I was working because I was having an affair with both the master *and* his eldest son, and their wives found out. A woman has a right to be happy so I did what I had to do to *be* happy. That meant that if I could not get what I wanted from the master, I got it from his son and vice-versa. For a while it worked and I managed to stash away quite a bit in jewelry and money -- as I never planned to remain a maid forever. But I got caught with the master late one evening and given the ultimatum from his wife, 'Her or me,' he chose her and I was made to leave before I could retrieve my money or treasures. After being forced out of the lavish life, as compared to some, that I was accustomed to enjoying, I have no useful skills to survive in any other capacity other than as a household maid. The master's and son's wives spread word of my infidelity with their husbands and now I would not be able to find work no matter how badly I should wish it. Destitute, I live wherever there is shelter, begging for handouts and stealing when it suits my needs. I saw this place one night after I was kicked out of the barn where I was staying and decided to come in. What of it? How did any of *you* find *your* way here? Were you born here?"

That story, which was not uncommon, and Ebony's nasty attitude satisfied most of the curious at the pub. She was not and had not been the first woman to be caught cavorting with both master and son. Many women had seen their way to the Dancing Dragon in times past, speaking of affairs with men of noble birth while in their employ and how they had been disgraced upon discovery.

To most of the tavern patrons, Ebony seemed as low classed as they were and a harlot to boot, so why should they question her? One woman however did continuously challenge Farayne's intricately crafted tale and she had grown weary of the whore's intentional nitpicking. The woman had tall stories of her own and did not like anyone who might actually have more of an interesting tale to tell than she did.

"And where was this, deary…this estate that you got kicked off of? I think you are lying!"

Farayne glared at the woman.

"Why would it matter to you, whore? Are you jealous because no one would allow a filthy, disgusting tramp like *you* on their estate? I wonder if every word that has slithered from *your* forked tongue that is the lie? It is *none* of *your* concern where the estate is located. Go back to stuffing your face. The noises you make while you chew are much more pleasant to hear than your voice!"

The woman's face turned red but she held her lying tongue in check. With a huff of indignant and arrogant anger that she only dreamed of being worthy enough to feel, she walked away. Tansy was watching and the whore knew it so she thought better of saying, let alone doing, anything to Ebony. That was that…the conversation was over.

Not much unlike the ill-reputed Dania and her exaggerated tales of who and what she had once been before her shame and shunning, Farayne had actually overheard the story she used on her own estate. Every word that she spoke had been due to eavesdropping on a deeply remorseful beggar woman who approached one of her maids one day while she was gardening. Farayne simply elaborated on her version a bit and added details that she had not actually overheard in the original telling.

Unbeknownst to her though, Farayne's stories were not the only thing people found interesting about her. She had been watched every night -- watched by people who had dark designs on her. This night they would make their move. They wanted to see if she would have such fire against them, if she would be able to protect herself from those who bade her far more harm than the fiery girl had ever encountered.

The tavern was closing and Farayne slipped silently away. She never tried to draw much attention to herself, either coming or going, especially going lest someone follow her home and see her for what she really was. If that were to happen she doubted that she would make it out of the pub alive again. Tall tales by whores were one thing, but a lady of means toying with the downtrodden of society as if they were some form of pathetic entertainment would not be tolerated.

Sometimes, as with the altercation with Tansy the prostitute when she first appeared at the small pub and the few times she'd had to defend her flawless skin and shining hair from those who were envious of her, being so noticeable couldn't be helped. Otherwise, she was happy just to sit quietly and observe.
She thought she had made it safely out of the tavern as she pulled her cape tighter about her to stave off the damp chill.

"Oy! 'aven't you been comin' 'ere every night? Why er you comin' 'ere? You don' belong 'ere pre'y miss!"

The man was grotesque. His teeth were missing, his hair was dirty, and he stank. He disgusted her. It was not that she thought herself better than him, as there were many at the tavern that looked just like him, but how difficult was it to bathe at least once a *week*? However, this man *was* different; there was something about him that unsettled her, more so than any of the other men whom she'd made contact with. Something told her that she was in danger. She looked him up and down and backed away. She continued backing up and backed into another man. When she turned around, she saw the man she had backed into was as horrible as the first. He had an eye patch and his breath nearly made her vomit. She realized as a wave of panic set in that she was surrounded. The men gazed at her as one would a jewel thrown carelessly out onto the street.

One of the men, she didn't see which because it happened so fast, grabbed her. The wind was knocked out of her as she was slammed onto the cold ground. She felt her heavy cotton tights ripped from her legs and her ragged petticoat torn away. The man began kissing her and she tried desperately to block him, but he held her tiny wrists in one of his huge hands. It was all she could do not to vomit. With each kiss, the man left wet *somethings* on her face that made her ill. She didn't wish to think about what was sticking to her face as his rough lips smeared her own lips and cheeks. She felt him rip her underwear from her and his dirty, stained and grubby fingers jam into her. She cried out in pain as he drove them repeatedly, deeply into her.

Suddenly he fell off her, or more accurately he *flew* off her. She coughed and sputtered as she regained her breath. All his weight had been on her and her ribs ached. The rest of the men had already run away and she saw her attacker scramble to his feet, pull up his pants and run away. It wasn't until then that she realized how close she had come to being savaged by the brute.

She stood on wobbly legs and then she saw it -- a shadow dashing into the forest. She tried to follow it but as quickly as it had come to her rescue, it disappeared. It had to be a man who saved her. Tansy was elsewhere…and not even *she* would come to her friend's rescue against such vagabonds, Farayne was certain. She knew that she had no real friends except for Tansy, so no one else had saved her; it had to be the shadow that dashed out of view that'd saved her. She didn't know who he was but she owed him her life, her virtue if nothing else. She vowed that she would find him and thank him.

Gathering her courage and never looking back, she ran for home.

Farayne was still winded from her run. She had literally run all the way home and by the time she made it to the back gate, she collapsed. She lay there, unconscious on the cold ground until the horses woke her. They were easily spooked so she wondered how long she had been unconscious and more importantly, if anyone had seen her. With the last of her strength, she trudged into the house and undressed. Her maid would fix her a bath first thing in the morning and she prayed that the rose-scented water would sufficiently cleanse the thug's nastiness from her. But in the meantime she would try to do what she could to keep from getting an infection.

Taking a clean cloth from the basin rack, she poured water into the bowl and dipped the cloth into it. The water was very cold and she shivered, but she washed herself carefully, cleansing an area of her body that had previously been mostly foreign to her. Oh she cleaned herself thoroughly for certain each time she bathed, but she had never had the opportunity to actually investigate what her body had to offer a future mate -- until now. She continued the cleansing, probing and wiping until she was sore.

Clean as she could get, but still feeling violated, she climbed into bed. She sighed and closed her eyes, the sheets pulled tightly up to her neck. That position proved to be an unwilling one to induce sleep, so she turned onto her side, a position that she had always found solace in. When she was sad, tired, or upset, turning on her side always offered her comfort and eventual sleep. However, even this night the cuddling of the heavy quilts and blankets could offer her no more than shelter from the chill. She simply could not get the feeling of the disgusting thug's fingers out of her. He had been so nasty, so disgustingly filthy; *how* would she explain to her maid *if* she got an infection that wasn't easily cured? She silently prayed that she wouldn't get one as she lay in her bed and thought of her savior and how she could find him and thank him for what he'd done.

54

FALLEN　　　VAN SCOYOC

Even while she lay in bed thinking of her mystery man, she felt the thug's fingers plunging painfully into her.

The last thought she had before she closed her eyes in a fitful sleep, was of the man who kept her from losing the most precious thing she had, and how she would never rest until she found him.

CHAPTER THREE
THE DANCING DRAGON REVISITED

Farayne pulled her cape about her and hard-set her jaw in determination as her destination came into sight. Nothing, nor *anyone*, would stop her from what she set out to do. She was not one to be foiled and she still needed to learn, she still had curiosities that needed slaking and until she was satisfied she would not stop. To a degree she couldn't help but feel sorry for the men who'd attacked her. What could drive a man to do such a thing to a young woman? Were the men really beasts? Were they mentally feeble? Had they been abused as children -- had a woman treated them so wrongly, so terribly as to make them hate women? So many questions filled her young mind that she scarcely heard the crude comments made to her by the tavern's inhabitants, the same sort of men who had attacked her. Most people left her alone, or faced Tansy's wrath, but every once in a while her friend was not around to watch over her. No matter. In the time she had been carrying on her masquerade, she'd learned things that life with the gentry could never have taught her. She giggled as she thought of what passed as insults in her world. How pathetic! Telling a man that his mother was a goat was bad? Not after what she had heard some of the men in the tavern say to others!

It had been a week since her attack at the hands of the ruthless barbarians who attempted to have their way with her. But she went back that next night, trembling, very frightened and extremely alert to her surroundings both coming and going. But she *had* gone back to the Dancing Dragon that next night, and the night after that. To her extreme relief the men who assaulted her were nowhere to be found. Their absence did not surprise her considering the terror with which they fled when her mystery hero stopped them, but she also knew that chances were something that humans, despite their intelligence or lack thereof, were willing to take if they thought the end result was worth that leap.

She thought again of him. She *had* to find him, no matter how long it took her.

Though she had thrown the torn petticoat, tights and underwear away, she was still wearing her ragged dress. The cape was a necessity, as the winds had turned colder in those passing days. She stood at the entrance to the pub for only a breath and then stepped inside.

Returning that first night was the most difficult for her. For a while she simply stood at the side of the building, shielded by the fragrant roses that climbed a nearby stone wall.

"Farayne, you can do this," she whispered quietly, "you can and you *will* do this! Now go in there and act as if nothing happened! These people, they are uneducated but they are not stupid. If they know what happened to you, or if those men are in there and know they frightened you, you will never get any peace from *any* of them! You cannot rely on your hero to save you again. Now go!"

The harsh pep talk she gave herself achieved the desired result and with head thrown high like the royalty she truly was, she walked through the door and to her table in the back.

She once again stood at the door and tossed her ebony locks over her shoulders, then stepped inside and hastened to her table.

She hadn't even gotten seated yet when she heard him — actually she smelled him first.

"Hey, little girl!"

Fear gripped Farayne in an icy embrace and she looked up. The man was grinning evilly at her. He was missing teeth too. What was it with these people?

"I can smell you and you smell good!"

She tossed her head in defiant arrogance. She knew by now that the man was *not* referring to the rose water she liberally splashed on herself...telling any who asked, that she had stolen it. She knew what he meant and it disgusted her.

"Unfortunately I can smell you too, dog, and *you do not* smell good. In fact, you smell as if a thousand donkeys have used you as their toilet!"

The man's face fell as his friends roared with laughter. Farayne looked up and Tansy was grinning at her. She winked and Farayne winked back. Relief flooded her. Maybe now the man and any others who wished to surprise her with their loose tongues and shocking statements would leave her alone. She did not expect Tansy to come to her rescue *every* time someone bothered her, but she felt better having the haggard old whore around.

With the thug humiliated into submission she smiled and relaxed into her chair for another night of interesting education at the Dancing Dragon.

It was closing time, or close thereof, she was sure of it. The old man, Bartles, always stayed until about closing time and he had just gotten up for his walk…more appropriately, stagger…home and many of the usual crowds had already left. The man whom Farayne had earlier beaten at his own game had bothered her no more that evening, but there were plenty more where he came from. She cut them all down with the same cool and calm haughtiness that she always possessed and they too quickly took their leave. She had taken a chance insulting the dregs, but she had to, or possibly be seen for what she really was -- a little girl playing a dangerous game -- and then all of her research would be for naught. She was so deep in thought as she sipped her ale, the ale that she still could not get a taste for, of her savior that she barely felt the soft tugging on her cape.

She ignored the tugging figuring it was another dreg wishing to lick, drink from or otherwise engage his rod with her lips – and not the ones on her face -- in some way. She wrinkled her nose as her mind raced through some of the disgusting things that she was propositioned each night to do.

Would her shadow be there for her if she were attacked again or would he simply leave her to the monsters, his sympathy having expired for a woman who should have learned her lesson

58

the first time? Though she had not seen him since that night she had the distinct feeling that he *was* there and watching her. The tugging became harder, insistent as if someone had something important to tell her.

She was almost afraid to turn around. Was it the thug she had insulted earlier, angry at being humiliated and then ignored -- drunk not only on the rough ale he imbibed, but also on the superhuman powers he believed it gave him? Was it the monsters that had attacked her, back to finish what they had started, hoping that her hero would not return to save her a second time? Farayne turned fearfully around and stared into the wise and wrinkled eyes of an old, old woman. This woman was no lady. She obviously had led a rough and dangerous life. Her face was lined and wrinkled beyond belief, unlike Farayne's own milky white skin, and her eyes were deep and hard set. She frightened the young woman.

"Deary you 'ave been comin' 'ere for the past month. What is it you seek 'ere? I know what 'appened to ye a few days ago. Don' ye think those men might come back? There are worse ones to be 'ad by too ye know? I can tell ye don' belong 'ere miss. Why do ye keep comin'?"

Farayne smiled kindly. This woman wouldn't harm her. She was simply curious.

"I continue to come here and *will continue to come here* because I must know why...why people choose to live this way. Why they do not try to better themselves. While in my lover's employ at the mansion where I worked, I saw the gatekeepers and household servants turn away people such as you for begging food and water. I do not understand why you feel you must beg when there could be *something* that could be bartered? I may not be much now, but I do try to better myself when I can. I see that many people here do not wish to better themselves; they desire only to survive. I must know when and why they stopped caring about themselves...about their lives."

The old woman smiled ruefully but her eyes belied her true knowledge. She was wise beyond all compare, and had lived enough experiences for ten lifetimes.

"Come dear, we will sit and talk in a corner where it is safer. No one will bother ye while with Old Aggie."

Farayne followed the stooped, dirty old woman to a dimly lit corner without question. With grunts and groans from a body that was worn and weary, the haggard crone sat down, Farayne alighting softly opposite her, her grace and fluidity obvious to the old hag. Farayne looked up to see that the woman had been right. The stares and shock on the faces of the people at the tavern suddenly melted as they quickly looked away from the duo. It was if they feared or even respected the ancient crone.

"I will tell ye me story, deary, and then ye will see why people fear me and others like me the way they do." The old women's eyes took on a different cast as she spoke. They shone brightly and then darkened and eventually they looked tired.
"I was not always a beggar woman. I was not always poor. I was born into wealth and privilege, such as yourself."

Farayne looked up, unable to help herself. The crone smiled.

"I knew ye was a girl of means the first time I laid eyes on ye, miss. That skin, that hair...though it may have escaped some, it did not escape me."

The crone patted Farayne's hand and continued. Farayne strained her ears over the din of the loud tavern to hear the quiet words the crone spoke. As her story unfolded she noticed that the hag's rough mannerisms seemed to melt away. She seemed educated and articulate. She was well-spoken and Farayne drank in every word that fell from the woman's withered lips.

"I was born to Lord Targin and Lady Jhanelle Ansington in the fall of fifteen-forty, in Leeds. I had the best of everything, but I was restless and never truly happy. I was always a different child. Though the cream of society I was shunned by my peers. Instead of dancing gaily with my friends, I preferred to read. I read everything I could get my hands on and soon became involved in witchcraft."

Farayne gasped.

The crone smiled and reached out to pat Farayne's hand in gentle reassurance once again.

"Oh nothing at all like *that*, deary. I practiced white magic only and used my knowledge to help people. I practiced in secret at first. I was too afraid of what would happen to me...to my family

60

or what my own blood would do to me if it were to ever become knowledge within my social class of my doings. The truth was, I felt more at home in nature and communing with God in His church, than going to a building and having someone give me their interpretation of what the Good Book means. While the few friends I had rode the countryside on their horses I chose to let my horse graze and walk beside her instead of riding her. To this day I can saddle a horse as well as any man. I used to practice on Sun Chaser, my horse, all the time. Though I never rode her I thought knowing how to saddle a horse might come in handy at some point in my life."

Farayne's eyes gleamed. Aggie rode a horse! At least she had at some point on her life. Farayne's mind began to spin. She could ride a horse too and although she'd never seen the importance before, now she did! Riding a horse *would* be of great benefit for her! She was so grateful that she'd actually learned how to do so! She could take one of the horses and ride away from her estate, much as Aggie had done hers!

The crone stopped and smiled for just a moment, as if sensing what her new young friend was thinking and then continued.

"While my peers had parties and coming out galas, I mixed spells and cured the beggars and simple country folk that would come to the manor for food and water. So many of them were sick and I knew I had to help them. Like you, I could not understand why, with all the money my parents had, they would not help the poor dregs.

I lived in secret -- but happily so -- for only a couple of years. To my undoing word got around about my *sorcery*. It was the very low-lifes I helped that caused my downfall.

It wasn't that those whom I had helped intentionally tried to ruin my life, just the opposite. In me they had found someone who cared, someone who would help people like them and in their zeal to sing my praises they told all they could that there was an angel of mercy amongst them. It did not take long for word to reach my home. My parents had people everywhere and in all manner of places to keep watch over me...*to ensure my safety they claimed*. I will never forget the day I was called to my father's meeting room. He had assembled my mother, my aunts and uncles and many of my elder cousins.

Before I even reached that hateful room I knew why I had been summoned. That walk down the long hallway to my father's all-important room was like walking to my own execution. At first I was terrified as I looked out at my family, their harsh eyes and menacing gazes tearing through me. Then, as I continued to await my doom, a sense of peace settled over me. It was as if the Creator was telling me that I had no reason to fear, that I would be all right. My father spoke words that I will never forget... 'No daughter of mine will you be from this day forward. You have communed with Lucifer and it is in his trust you now go. You are stripped of every birthright you possess and if you ever return to this manor again, I will personally have you killed. The service of the Lord Jesus Christ is what we desire, not the devil's consort. All in agreement say 'aye.'

I watched as each of my family members said 'aye.' My mother was the last. She said 'aye' and then ran screaming, sobbing hysterically, from the room.

I said nothing to my defense. There was nothing to say. I knew my family would not understand that the magic I worked was in the name and for the glory of our Lord Christ, not the devil. I knew they would not comprehend what they did not wish to understand. I turned and walked out of my home, right out of that room, down the hallway, through the foyer and out the front door. My father followed me...he knew that I was heading toward the stable.

I wanted nothing from my life and nothing from my home except my horse. *She had found me* one day while I was in a beautiful field picking herbs for spell working. Sick and eaten up with sores I could almost hear her begging my help. She was *mine and I was hers* - not a gift and she was not purchased. She chose me and I do not know what I would have done had my father taken her away from me.

It was my intention to simply leave all that I had ever known even though I knew not where I would go or what I would do, and set off into the woods. In his only act of mercy, my father did allow me to take Sun Chaser with me and having her gave me more comfort than I can put into words. Had he thought her worth anything I am certain he would have kept her or sold her. However I know my father and how he thought. If she was mine and I was the devil's concubine then she was evil too and he would not want her on his property. At the time she was truly the only friend I had. We walked until near sunset and just as the sun was sinking into the black of night, I found a tiny, run down cottage. It was dark and I could not see well, but I chanced inside and found it abandoned, or at least it appeared to be. I don't think I fully slept that night, although I knew Sun Chaser would let me know if anyone untoward bothered either of us.

With dawn's first light I awoke and inspected the cottage. It was a mess and cobwebs were so thick they bathed the room in a white glow. The furniture was broken or rotted and the roof had a leak in it. However, I loved it and saw it as a challenge to make it completely mine. It was obvious that no one had been there in a long time.

I worked hard on the little shack and soon it was beautiful…at least in my eyes it was. Unlike the manor I had grown up in, this shack was *mine* and I made it truly *my own*. I prayed daily that no one would come and lay claim to it, but if they did, I was prepared for that too.

My communing with nature had served me well and soon my cottage had a new thatched roof. That I could do on my own, but other things I needed a little help with. I went to town, trading the jeweled pin from my hair for the seeds and other staples that I needed to grow my own garden and make my own bread. Poor Sun Chaser was over-laden with all that I bought, but I carried my share too and promised her that this would be the first and last time she would be a beast of burden. She seemed to understand and made not even one protest on the way home.

The seeds I bought, and then planted in the Creator's name by the light of the first full moon, served me well and soon I had a lovely garden. Until my garden matured fully I knew that I could live off the wild nuts and berries I had all around me. The forest was a treasure trove of delicious berries of all kinds, and nourishing nuts. Many days Sun Chaser and I would share a handful of both after a walk. In what seemed like no time at all, my garden flourished and I was so very proud of it. Without my parents' knowledge I had at one time grown a wonderful garden and knew I could survive on what I could cultivate from the land. With the axe I bought to cut wood when necessary, as I prefer to use fallen branches when I can, I had all the firewood I could ever need for cooking and spell working. My new life had begun and I was very excited. No more royal parties, no more of my father's cold and uncaring eyes. I was on my own…as I had always preferred it.

I lived simply and very happily on my own and knew that I had found true peace. If Heaven could be attained on earth I had found a bit of it in my own little corner.

Sun Chaser and I walked the countryside every morning and loved the quiet solitude of the early day just as the world was waking up. I found the fog that surrounded me comforting. I would pull my cape tightly about me and pick wildflowers to put in the small vase I kept on my kitchen table. That table meant the world to me. A young man made it for me as payment when I cured his sick baby. The baby needed medicine and because the man and his wife, who was barely a teenager, were poor the doctor would not see them. The baby had a cough deep in its tiny chest and would surely have died had it not been for me. I mixed up a potion for the infant and soon it was happy and healthy again. I did nothing out of the ordinary and it cost me nothing to do…the same thing it would have cost the doctor in town had he simply had the decency to do it. When those parents brought that smiling babe back to see me a week later, it was all I could do not to cry. I have never grown tired of helping people for just that reason. The expression on a person's face when you have saved their life or the life of a loved one is simply more than my heart can describe.

My life may seem to have been lonely, but it was far from being so. I had the whole of the world at my back door and though my friends were all four-legged, I never lacked for any of them. Woodland creatures visited me daily and birds sang to me the most angelic of music.

I loved to walk and I walked everywhere no matter how far the journey might be. One morning I was out with Sun Chaser walking the vast valley by our home, picking flowers and as I picked the last flower for my bouquet, I looked up to see a handsome young man on a horse. He was staring at me curiously. I smiled and nodded in greeting and he dismounted. He too was a person of class; that much was obvious from his elegance and manner of dress. I could tell right away that like I had, it seemed that he too longed to be away from the constraints of court life. There is just something in the eyes of a person who is unhappy…the expression is unmistakable. We spoke for a while and it was then that I learned I had been right about him. His morning rides were the only solace he had away from his father grooming him to take his place as head of household. We met in secret each morning and walked the countryside getting to know each other little by little. He was guarded at first, as a man in his position should be, but when I told him who I was, *who and what I had been…*and how I came to be an outcast, I could see the relief wash over his face. He was not alone in the world and was happy to find that there were kindred spirits away from court.

No one ever found out about us and we spent every moment we could together. We soon discovered that we were deeply in love. He asked me many times to marry him and every time I refused. He was a man of distinct royalty, even more so than I had been, and though I never regretted my decision to give up everything I knew for the life I lived, I could not, *would not* ask anyone else to do the same. What if later in life he felt that he had made a mistake?

No matter how I dissuaded him, he left his title, the lands that would have been his after his father's passing, and like I had, all that he knew to be with me. It made no matter that we were both of royal blood. I was an outcast and if he wished to be with me he would be outcast as well. We married six months after we met and were married for fifty-five years, raising six wonderful children -- five boys and one girl. The good Lord called him home ten years ago and I miss him just as much today as I did the day I saw him on his way to his new home in the sky. I still live in my cottage, *our* cottage, and am very happy. I miss my beloved husband terribly, but he will *always* be with me.

Even after losing my husband, even if all were forgiven and forgotten…even if I *could*, I *would never* go back to the life I grew up with. That life is foreign to me; it always was I suppose. The life I have lived for most of my teenaged and adult years is the only life I choose to live. I come here to this tavern to simply be with people, as I am lonely. I like people; I just never had anything in common with the boors of my peers. I have nothing in common with these folk either, but I simply wish not to be alone. As one's mortality looms, you find that being around *anyone* is a comfort…at least it is to me. Oh these people are rough, as you have seen and they can be cruel, but if you break through the tough exterior they have they are simply common folk with no education or upbringing. It is true that the people here fear me to some degree. Maybe I have led them to believe that my practicings are a little more devilish than what they are, but that is for my own safety. You have seen, first hand, what can happen to a woman in a place such as this."

The old crone's eyes sparkled. Farayne could not help but admire her. She had the courage to leave a life of immense comfort and wealth for a life of rough living and no money, and all because it made her happy. How she wished she could do the same thing! "Now young miss, do you understand why I told you my story?"

Farayne smiled.

"Yes. Our people fear those less fortunate because they are still we to some degree. Nothing is forever and at any moment you can have everything taken from you. I do not feel that you lost anything though, Aggie. You had the courage I lack to seek your heart's desire. I admire you and wish I had your spirit."

The crone smiled and patted the girl's head.

"You have the courage, young miss. You just have not tapped into it yet! Listen to your heart. You will find happiness, or I should say, it will find you when you least expect it!"

How ironic, Farayne thought. Her father had said the same thing many times, but it never made her feel as good as hearing Aggie say it. Farayne knew that it was because her father was not thinking of her happiness in the same way Aggie was when he spoke those words. His idea of happiness was for her to get married and give him a house full of grandchildren.

"Now miss, you must get back home. It is past closing time and if you are who I believe you to be, you have a long walk ahead of you...Lady Gleneden."

Once again, Farayne's eyes snapped up from her daydream into the tired but wise eyes of her new friend.

The ancient crone winked. Farayne kissed her withered cheek and with a squeeze of her weathered and work-worn hand disappeared from the tavern.

The night looked anew as Farayne walked along. She had always appreciated the darkness, but after hearing Aggie's story, she saw everything much clearer. The night seemed alive to her and where shadows had always frightened her a little, now she felt as though she could walk *with* them instead of away from them. She felt happier than she ever had. The ancient crone's story had given her hope and ideas. *She* could grow a garden! *She* could have the stable boys show her how to saddle a horse! *She* could read books and look for herbs! How wonderful this new life would be for her! A rustling behind her whirled her around. She was suddenly very frightened. Feelings of dread that she had almost mercifully forgotten came creeping over her. She was almost too terrified to move.

"Who is there? Show yourself!" she demanded with a confidence she far from felt.

"You have no need to fear me."

The voice was gentle and Farayne relaxed somewhat. Out from the shadows stepped a devastatingly handsome man. With tumbling black hair, ebony eyes, and lily-white skin, he looked to be more wraith than man. Farayne thought him beautiful. Never had she seen such a specimen of human!

"Who…who are you?"

"I am Garrison Maxwell, my Lady. I mean you no harm."

Farayne was instantly smitten.

"How do you know me?"

"I have been following you home from the Dancing Dragon Pub for the past month. A lady such as yourself should not be consorting with such lowlifes."

Farayne was flattered. Never had the young men she'd encountered in her social circles spoken such lovely words to her and in such an eloquent manner. Her heart fluttered. Could this dark spirit be her savior, the man who had so quickly disappeared after helping her?

"I must ask you sir and please, I ask that you tell me the truth. Are you the gentleman who saved me from being taken at the pub that night by those horrid men?"

The man was silent for a moment and when he answered it was final, as if he wished to discuss what he had done no further.

"Yes."

Farayne's heart danced. This man entranced her! The men she knew, the men of her circles and the men that her father continuously tried to push her off to, would have expected medals and parties and would have basked in the "honorable deed" they had done for months! Yet this man expected nothing for his heroic deed.

"I cannot thank you enough, sir. I shudder to think what those characters would have done to me had it not been for your intervention."

The man shrugged.

"Think nothing more of it. I did nothing that any other gentlemen would not have done. Please, allow me to walk you home."

Farayne's mouth went dry. Could this really be happening? This man wanted to walk her home?

"Yes. Thank you," she managed to weakly croak.

Like the perfect gentlemen he seemed to be, he motioned for her to walk ahead and he fell in step beside her. Farayne could not explain it, but she felt completely at ease with this man, yet she knew nothing about him. How did she know that he was not the same type of man, like those who tried to have their way with her outside the pub? How did she know that he would not do worse to her than anything she could imagine? She didn't, yet something told her that she was safe. She had absolutely no fear of this mesmerizing specter and did not think twice about allowing him to walk with her.

The walk home ended much too quickly for the lovely lady and she stood at the gate for a long while watching the shadows of the night engulf her new friend until he was no longer visible. He had not come from the swirling mist of her morning time dreams, he was not engulfed in the gray fog that she'd so often envisioned her ideal man being cocooned in -- he had come from the night, out of shadow. He had not come specifically for her, rather yet by accident they had met...but that was good enough for her. She didn't know how but she knew that she had to get to know this dark angel more than what a walk home could provide her with.

CHAPTER FOUR
GARRISON

Garrison was all that Farayne could think about. Though she had not seen him for a few nights she felt as if he were nearby. She could not explain the feeling of being watched. It was not an uncomfortable feeling but more like a reassuring reminder that safety was not far.

But Farayne did something that she had never done before and something that she certainly was not accustomed to -- she began to doubt herself and her savior's actions. Maybe he was simply being kind to her that night he walked her home and she was reading entirely too much into his deed. No matter, she wished to know more about him and she would not stop until her curiosity was satisfied or he insisted upon his leave from her.

The trip to the Dancing Dragon seemed to take no time at all and as she walked along, her thoughts were not of the continuing education she was receiving, but of her lovely savior. She heard rustling behind her again as she wondered what she would say to him if she were to see him.

"I had hoped that you would not return there, my lady."

Farayne wheeled and broke into a broad smile.

"Garrison!"

Garrison cocked his head and bowed in mock humility. He did not seem the type to smile, but for a brief second Farayne saw the corner of his lip turn up in amusement.

Farayne clasped her hands in front of her, her fingers interlaced so tightly it was painful. Never had she felt so awkward in front of anyone. It was normally others who behaved in such a manner around her and now she saw how it felt to be shy, unsure and nervous.

"I…I was not going to the Dancing Dragon for the company, Garrison…I was going in hopes of seeing you again."

Garrison's only response to such a flattering statement was to raise his left eyebrow. Farayne's heart sank. She bowed her head and waited for him to tell her what a foolish child she was and that she would never see him again. The words never came so she slowly lifted her head. He was standing right in front of her! How had he managed to move so swiftly without her seeing it? She chanced a look even higher at his handsome face. Once again, his lip was curled in a smirk.

"Then see me you shall. You are seeing me now. Do you wish to speak with me as well, or just gaze at me?"

Normally Farayne would have tossed her head in spoiled rebuff and stomped away at such a sarcastic remark, but she did not. She not only wished to see her dark angel, but she wished to speak with him as well about anything and everything he desired. Just being in his presence was enough for her but even better if she actually had someone intelligent to speak with. .

"If I may do both, I would find it quite pleasing."

Garrison extended his arm and she wrapped her tiny hand around it. Off they trekked into the night.

Farayne saw Garrison every night after that meeting. He was kind to her and seemed to enjoy her company, though he was a man of very few words. She didn't mind as what he did not say with words his eyes vocalized. She was intrigued by his elegant mannerisms, his eloquent and often highly intelligent speech, and his graceful but subdued actions. He was a perfect gentleman and always made her feel like a real person, not some trophy to be had to raise one's social standing. All she had ever wanted from her peers was respect and yet that was the one thing that neither man nor woman would give her. She was simply *strange* to her social circle of young women, and a beautiful piece of jewelry to the young men who vied for her hand.

She spoke openly with Garrison, telling him of her desire to be rid of life at court and the feelings of languishing in tired propriety forever.

"I have started skipping teas, and not one of them do I miss. If I thought I could have gotten away with it I would have started skipping them years ago. I have returned the few social invites that find their way to my door and do not miss those either. I have never been terribly conspicuous at them so I doubt I am missed. If anything I give the gossips even richer fodder than before. Now they can speak about me all they wish and not have to worry about minding their manners when I walk back into the room. My father is not happy, but he need not concern himself with anything but his own affairs. However, that is my father…he must rule everything and everyone. Sometimes I think my mother was fortunate in her passing. I can only imagine how he plagued her every step, shadowed her every waking moment and eavesdropped on her every word. I simply did not realize until I was older just how much of a menace he is."

Garrison's lip turned up again.

"Are you not being a little harsh on your father?"

Farayne's eyebrows lifted sharply in defiance. Garrison smiled -- a full smile -- and then continued. "I understand your desire to be rid of such boring wastes of time. I never understood the use of a tea, but then again, I'm sure that women do not understand the use of the hunt either."

Farayne huffed in indignation.

"Oh I most certainly do…so men can brag about exploits they have either never done or that they wish to do and would like to start bragging early. It is a men's tea…different sides of the same coin," she intoned.

"Indeed."

Garrison was amused by his beautiful guest's outspoken nature though she could not see that amusement as she brashly proclaimed her opinion. It was not something that women did, speaking out and yet this bundle of independence was a ball of fire and obviously one that would be difficult to contain should be put even a small bit of effort into obtaining what she desired. She was so much different than the women he was used to. She was a nice change for him and he enjoyed her company. He would have never imagined being in the company of a woman with heart, but also one that knew what she wished in life and was not afraid to strive toward it.

Farayne had thoughts of her own that would surprise her host and hadn't told Garrison that she had begun ridding herself of the young men who wished her attentions, in addition to the haughty peers of her sociality. She did not wish to seem brash and did not want to scare him away by having him think that she was wishing to rid herself of suitors in hopes that he would have her for his own, though that was exactly what she wished. No...no matter how much she desired to be in his company and to just *be with him*, she would not allow him that knowledge. She would simply work with what she had and pray that he would come to love her for her many wonderful attributes on his own, with no treachery from her.

Farayne sighed inwardly. Suitors...oh what a vexing problem they were! They had been more difficult to get away from, but she managed to find ways around seeing them. She would feign headaches, female problems the likes of which she would have gladly gone into detail about had it been necessary to rid herself of the more stubborn ones. That had never been necessary though, much to her chagrin. She smiled inwardly at the thought that if word spread about what an indecent woman she was, speaking of matters to a man that were better kept between women, maybe the remaining clinging suitors would have gladly left her alone.

She made certain that for the more despicable men, she would *forget* appointments with them and soon the suitors, even the ones her father tried so desperately to set her up with, stopped coming to see her.

As the two people sat and talked for the remainder of the night, Farayne did tell Garrison of a wish she had and hoped that he would not be angry with her.

She wished to return to the Dancing Dragon one last time, to see Aggie. Farayne had learned all that she needed to know while at the pub, at least what she had set out to learn and needed not to return -- except to bid her dear old friend farewell. Her curiosity was finally fulfilled, and while she had enjoyed herself, if she could spend her time with Garrison she would much prefer to do that.

Garrison's eyes seemed troubled for a brief moment and

then haltingly, he agreed, his ebony hair falling in his face as he slowly nodded.

Farayne could tell that her decision to return to such a den of lowliness was not a very popular one with her new friend but she felt it only fair to Aggie and she needed to bid Tansy, as despicable as she was and what she did ungodly, farewell too.

Farayne looked up at the sign outside the pub. What once seemed like a beacon to her had now lost its glory. The marker that had given her comfort so many times as she stepped from the gloom of the woods, beckoning her to safety, was nothing more than a simple wooden sign now. It had lost its allure as the enticement of a long awaited adventure. Garrison refused to go inside but vowed that he would not be far from her in case she needed his help.

Farayne looked back at Garrison one last time before she went inside and he nodded to her. She suddenly felt more confident and with head held high, stepped inside. Tansy was the first to greet her and the bartender immediately poured her a drink. Thanking him, she took it and scanned the crowd, spotting Aggie at the back of the tavern, an old pipe in her hand and a small pint before her. As she approached her friend she breathed in the aromatic smoke that swirled around the old woman, a tantalizing scent that she was certain was Aggie's own blend of tobacco.

"My dear! You have come back to see me!"

"Yes, Aggie. I have come to see you and I have brought a friend though he is shy. He is around, but not where you can see him."

The crone seemed overjoyed at seeing the lovely lady again and she and the once-important socialite talked until close.

Farayne smiled and Aggie nodded her balding head.

"I knew you'd found someone, my dear girl, I could feel it in my soul that you were happy. Planning on leaving home are you?"

Farayne was pleased that Aggie spoke with elegance and intelligence in her presence. Though Farayne planned a life of earthen living just like Aggie, the one thing she would not compromise on was her education. She smiled as she looked carefully at her tired friend. Once again Farayne was shocked at the ancient hag's intuition. How could she have known that since their first conversation, she had been planning just that? Cutting off her already small circle of supposed friends was merely the first step.

"Aggie…you amaze me! After our very first conversation I decided that I would leave my home and move out away from everything and everyone. Your story inspired me. I can grow a garden, I can learn to take care of myself."

Aggie removed her pipe from her crusty lips and winked at the young girl.

"You still have much to learn though, missy. Make certain that you study as many books as you can and try everything out to make certain you can do it before you simply up and leave the comfort of home. Luckily I studied hard and tried everything I could before I was disowned. Home may not be perfect at this time, but it is better than starving.

If you try and fail come to me and I will teach you all that I know. My children are all successful; my boys all work farms and have nice homes and my daughter is a dressmaker, catering to the wealthy and elite. She has money and a nice cottage. They don't need my sort of knowledge so when I die, all the knowledge I have tucked away in my brain, which someone might find valuable, will die with me. I would like to pass what I know on to *someone*. I can think of no one better than you."

Farayne squealed with joy and threw her arms around the crone, crying happily. Aggie smelled terrible, but Farayne didn't care. Hearing that Aggie would even entertain the idea of teaching her was more than she could have dreamed of. She had mulled over and over in her mind how she could ask the learned woman to teach her, without insulting her and as if reading her mind, Aggie offered just what she hoped for.

"You have just answered my prayers, Aggie. I would love to learn from you."

Aggie nodded.

"I live in the cottage on the far side of Clark Forrest. Come see me anytime. Except for the night, I am always home with my cat Charon."

Farayne smiled, her cheeks still wet with tears.

"I will my dear friend…I will."

The days and nights passed into weeks and the weeks into months and Farayne enjoyed life more than she ever had. She no longer had frivolous parties to attend and her suitors, much to her father's disappointment, were gone never to be heard from again. The only thing that Farayne lamented was that she and her father had begun fighting. He was very angry over her refusal to attend parties and her crude manners at missing important engagements that he had gone to great pains to set up for her.

No matter how she tried to explain her desire to choose her own husband and to avoid the hateful gossips that she had so loosely called "friends," he simply did not understand. His voice thundered in unholy wrath as he bellowed the excuse that his pairing with her mother had been arranged by their respective fathers. It was common practice within their class so as to have the best mate possible and was never to be given any thought; it was simply expected. Much to her parent's relief, they had many things in common and fell deeply in love. But their story was not a common one and Farayne knew it. How many times had she overheard the tearful lamentations of her mother's friends when they came to visit, speaking of cold and cruel or distant and apathetic husbands? She knew that she could never hope to be so lucky in her husband as her mother had been, or at least as she considered herself to be, in that she might actually love the man her father would choose for her. No matter whether it was for her own good or not money and power did not equal a good husband and father…and she certainly would not be happy if her husband were to be Ronan Tanserlyn!

Farayne grew more and more disillusioned with her home life as the arguments between she and her father became more and more frequent, escalating to him threatening to cut her out of his life, to her throwing things at him. She spent more and more of her days in Aggie's tutelage and the nights with Garrison. If it took her a lifetime to gain this man's love, she would wait.

Home was simply unbearable.

Garrison took Farayne to his house one evening instead of taking her home after their nightly walk. She was thrilled that he had begun to open up to her. He seemed to speak freely now instead of being so guarded. She could tell that he trusted few and this gesture, taking her to his home…his last sanctuary of privacy, was a momentous one. How she wished he would tell her why he spoke so little of himself but she would not ask. When Garrison was ready to talk to her in the manner she wished him to, he would. He opened the door standing back and motioned for her to go inside, bowing as she walked past him. Each time he performed such an act, her spine tingled and she giggled.

Farayne marveled at her love's home, a stylish but quaint country manor. It was neither pretentious nor showy but it was elegant. It was filled not with shallow and meaningless art and statues like her own home, but rather with objects of interest that, when she inquired as to their origin, he claimed to have picked up in his many travels.

Farayne knew that Garrison had seen the world, as he had mentioned so in passing one evening, and she longed to hear of his travels. He rarely said more than necessary in answer when she questioned him, preferring to hear more of her interests, thoughts, hopes, goals and dreams. It was as if it gave him pleasure to hear her speak. While she appreciated such kindness -- her former peers could prattle on for hours about themselves -- his lack of conversation about himself made getting to know him difficult. As it were, she knew virtually nothing of *him* compared to what he knew of *her*. It seemed as if she had told him her entire life's story and to a degree, she supposed she had. Farayne was only too happy to tell Garrison whatever he wished to know about her. She had no secrets and her life was uneventful. She couldn't deny that, for a change, it was nice to have someone ask her about *her*, what *she* wanted out of life and *actually care*. She hoped that as she spoke more of herself he would do the same.

The men she had been raised around could (and oftentimes did) talk endlessly about themselves, displaying a totally indifferent attitude when they *finally* asked about their female companion's day, hopes or even life in general. Even when they did ask, they spent the time either making eye contact with their friends and looking the suave and debonair part as if to say 'Look at me and whom I am with!' or incessantly interrupting to speak more of themselves. She loathed hearing their boring tales and glassed up stories of deeds they either could not have done, or invented just so they would have no one to question the validity of their heroic claims.

"Were you there? I think not, you coward, so how dare you question my statement! While you were home reading, lazing about or simply being useful to *no one*, I was out making a difference in the world. How regretful that you cannot say the same!" filled the air at each gala she attended as the men sought to 'out-sport' one another. It angered her how presumptuous the men of her social circles could be. They thought that if they told the same tale over and over that some poor fool would believe them!

Garrison was so different from those men. He would say nothing to her beyond what was required, almost as if fearing that she would think him boastful. Boastful? That was the last thing this charming man was! He was as humble and reserved as she had ever seen. She so wished that he would not fear speaking to her. She ached to learn more about him and hoped that with time he would fill her head with his fanciful stories.

So far he had told her he was the only child of a Scottish duke, Gandarwyn Maxwell and his wife, Duchess Elsabet Urquhart, a duchess in her own right even before she married his father. Like she and her new friend Aggie, Garrison had shunned his royal

78

upbringing, leaving home to see the world at the age of seventeen. He never returned for any length of time to his ancestral home on the Isle of Skye, much to the disappointment of his parents. The last time he visited his home was when his mother died. He was not warmly received. The rest of his family had never forgiven him for breaking his parent's hearts by deserting them.

After his father's death, Garrison making it to his father's bedside only after his passing, it was expected that he would take the title and stand in representation of his family. He refused, leaving right after the funeral to the angry shouts and insults of his family. In his stead, his Uncle Indirin had taken the title. The Duke knew how his only child felt about court life and though he prayed his son would change his mind, he had a feeling that Garrison *would* refuse the honor. In the event that such a disgraceful action as negating his family duty came to pass, he had an obligation to preserve their family history. It was written that Indirin would take the title and he had. However, his rule was short lived as he contracted an illness and died shortly after his crowning. Being so much younger than his brother Gandarwyn -- Garrison's age to be exact -- Indirin had not taken a wife nor had he sired any children. The title of 'Duke of the House of Tronquin' died out with him. The family had never forgiven Garrison and they never would. His refusal to take up his birthright and the subsequent problems that arose because of that refusal, found the title wrongfully thrust upon his naïve uncle, a man that was not suitable for such a responsibility.

Now, Garrison traveled and wrote memoirs that he hoped to publish one day. He let Farayne read a few of them and they were fascinating. What an exciting life he had led, sailing the seas with pirates, traveling the English countryside by horse, studying the ways of the Orient with wise Chinese masters, and exploring the countrysides of ancient Greece! Farayne hoped that she could one day see the things that he had seen, and more.

Farayne hated to leave Garrison's house that first night, as she felt more at home there than she did at her own home and longed to spend as much time as she could with him. She also wished not to think on the brewing storm that awaited her at home...

It had not been that long since that first night they met, but she found that she had fallen so deeply in love with her handsome savior that she would do anything...*anything* to simply have him love her. While she had actually fallen in love with him that night he walked her home, she was terrified to even hint at such a revelation. She had never been rejected, not by anyone and not for any reason. Garrison seemed to need no one, not a woman to keep his bed warm, or even to keep him company and she would not know what to do if he rejected her. She could have any man of court she wished -- yet she wanted none of them. She simply wanted one man, and that was the man she probably could never have. Farayne refused to give up though and hoped that Garrison would return her feelings eventually. She would wait. She had nothing better to do and no one better to wait for.

CHAPTER FIVE
REVELATIONS AND FEELINGS

Farayne continued to treasure each night...*each moment* that she spent with Garrison. He seemed to appreciate every little thing he saw around him, unlike the men of court who took everything and *everyone* for granted. In return, Farayne found that she too had been gifted with a new appreciation of life, something that she never knew she could feel. It amazed her how much negativity had influenced her attitude and heart and she was so pleased to be encircled by light and joy instead of pomp and anxiety. It seemed with each visit that she was breaking down her love's seemingly impenetrable walls and she became nearly giddy with hope.

As they walked the countryside by the bright light of the full harvest moon one evening, impulse overtook her and she hugged him. She expected him to pull away or at least gently admonish her, but he did neither. Instead he slipped his arm around her. His feelings soon became evident, but in a way that Farayne could never have imagined.

After a lovely, quiet dinner one evening, as the fire crackled in the fireplace and the shadows stretched long into the darkness, he bared his soul to her. Never could she have prepared herself for what he was going to tell her. She encouraged him to talk freely as she wished to know *anything* that he had to tell her. The words that fell from his pale lips were a symphony of heavenly sounds and she would hang on every syllable.

As he began his tale she prayed so hard he would tell her that he loved her.

Garrison began slowly at first, and then as he spoke the words came easier. Farayne did indeed hang on every word vowing not to miss one breath of his tale.

"My dear, I have told you that I was born a noble, on the Isle of Skye, but I never told you *when* I was born. I was born in the year 1011."

Farayne's eyebrows shot up in surprise but Garrison continued, oblivious to her reaction, as if he feared that if he stopped he might not be able to continue.

"Yes, I know, the year is 1620 now. You wonder how it can be possible that I was born six hundred and nine years ago and yet here I sit, with you? It is possible because I am not a mere man you see. I am no longer mortal. I am vampyre, a legion of the damned, cursed to walk the Earth until time holds no sway."

Garrison stopped and looked into his sweet companion's eyes, almost as if begging her not to run away from him.

Farayne knew that she should be terrified, but she couldn't be. Vampyres didn't really exist did they? She had often heard tales of the dark and beautiful ones who roamed the countryside at night, some doing unspeakable things to those they met and many others helping anyone in need. It was difficult to discern what to believe and what to dismiss as fairytale, stories told to frighten naughty children. Obviously Farayne had met one of the kind ones and she wished Garrison to continue with his tale. She would not miss one second of hearing his life story.

"Please continue, my sweet Garrison. I am neither frightened of you, nor ashamed to be in your presence. You intrigue me and your adventures are more than I can even imagine in my small and secluded world. Please…*please tell me more*!"

It seemed to take a moment for her words to register, almost as if the beautiful man could not believe what he had heard…and then he smiled.

"As you wish, my dear Farayne. I was brought across in the year 1031, while traveling with the pirates I have spoken of. I was quite naïve when it came to the ways of the world, and never had I seen such sights as I traveled with my newfound friends! Court life was much different than what the real world had to offer me. I realized that while a noble in my own country, in the world outside of Scotland, I was a non-entity…I meant nothing in the lives of the people I encountered. My title, had I taken it, would have served me naught in the world that awaited me.

The men of my party robbed and raped freely. I never raped, I did not believe in such atrocities against a woman, but the others did not share my respect of the female breed. We drank, we plundered, and I lived like a king, without the constraints of a royal court watching my every move. It was an existence that I liked and could have learned to love possibly, had I taken up with a different sort of people. The life I had become a part of did do me one service…it showed me just how inconvenient my naiveté was…and how it would contribute to my downfall.

I met her in a pub much like the Dancing Dragon. We were in a small town in Italy, the name escapes me now, but the port was beautiful as was the town and its inhabitants. Gentle and lovely people they all were. Pious and humane, I would have stayed there if I could, as I had never in my life been exposed to such an enchanting group of people.

I was twenty years old, a virgin, and very shy around women, so it was no surprise that I took a great deal of teasing from my friends. I was the butt of many jokes but I did not mind. They were pirates, uneducated, crude, rude and unkempt. It was not their fault; they simply did not know better. My virginity was something that I was not ashamed of…I did not know I was supposed to be. It had always been expected that my parents would choose a mate for me so I never had to interact with women, on any level."

Farayne cringed as Garrison spoke, thoughts bursting to the surface of her mind that she was trying so hard to forget.

"She bewitched me from the first night I saw her, dark and mysterious. She turned every head in the pub, and exuded an aura of complete mystery. Not until much later would I learn why she set her sights on me and on all of us in my party. We drank with her, we talked to her and many of my friends shared her bed. How I wished I could catch her eyes, but what did I know of pleasing a woman? I did not wish to have her laugh at me or humiliate me before my friends because of my lack of prowess in her bed, so I did nothing but worship her from as far away as I could.

One by one the men in my traveling company began to disappear. The captain, certain they were deserting, cursed them all as worthless and ordered that we would set sail for Ireland by the end of the week. That was all the time she, Isabella was her name, needed to finish what she had set out to do.

One foggy night, after too much drink, and feeling surer of myself than I normally did, she seduced me and I allowed her to. I was still awkward and no matter the amount of drink I had, nothing could change that. All it took was one look into her mesmerizing eyes and I would have followed her to the ends of the Earth. I took her that night in a rage of passion that left me begging for more. She laughed and pushed me away, telling me that if I were 'a good boy' for her, she would allow me to take her again. I must have pleased her to a degree, as I took her again and again that night and many nights after.

Little did I know that she had been using me, using the entire crew of the ship, to feed her bloodlust. You see -- she was a vampyre, a wicked, evil bitch of darkness, who intended to take not only our bodies, but also our souls.

Our last night together, as we lay in each other's arms after our ravenous coupling, I begged her to come with me. I loved her and I could not imagine life without her. She laughed at me. I should have seen it then, but I was so blinded by lust and what I believed to be love, that any warning my brain tried to give me was stampeded by the feelings in my heart. I should have left her then, but I did not...I could not...*I would not.*

I had never told *anyone* who I really was but if it meant that she might love me, I decided to use my birthright to my advantage. Never before had I cared about my birthright and did not care about it then either, but if it would make this ravishing creature mine, then I would gladly use it! I may have had nothing to offer her in Italy, but in Scotland I could give her anything she wished. With a powerful woman by my side, I could and would take up the title and make the most of court life.

'I am but a mere boy in *your* eyes, my darling Isabella, but the truth be known, I am a noble by birth, a Duke with a title, and quite well to do. I can and will give you everything you wish, if you will simply be my bride.'

I *knew* that I could make her happy, I simply had to convince *her* of it. Her eyebrows shot up in surprise. The look in her eyes…it was unmistakable. She had seduced someone who might possibly have people looking for him, or who might have connections that would lead them to her.

Once again, I missed any and all warnings with which to save my body and soul.

'Are you now, my dear babe? Hmm….money. Now what would I do with money?'

She laughed and then continued on, 'I like power, and money will come in time. For you see, my sweet, I already have power, and I can have money anytime I wish. So tell me…*why* would I need you?'

Once again she laughed wickedly at me, as she often did, and this time her laugh hurt me to my soul. She was indeed laughing *at* me, something she had never done so openly before. She had *always* laughed at me but cleverly disguised it by being coy and charming. When she laughed at me *that* night, it was cruelty and hard-heartedness in her words that mocked me. I was not sure what to make of her statement. She had power for certain; every man that gazed upon her pledged his soul to her…was she speaking of some other power? She smirked at me and then furiously, kissed my neck. Even when I felt the pinch of her teeth sinking into my skin I did not realize what was happening. Looking back now, I am afraid that even if I had known of her plans for me, I was so blinded by my love for her that I would have allowed her to do what she wished to me…and she did. She drained me of nearly all my blood and then tossed me aside like a toy she no longer wanted. By the time she finished with me I was near death and heartbroken. I begged her to tell me what I had done to incur such hateful treatment from her. Had she asked for my blood, my body -- whatever she wanted, I would have gladly given it to her. She had no need to attack me in the savage manner in which she did. The words she spoke were like a dagger in my heart.

'How could *I* love a little boy such as yourself? I have killed more men than you will ever see! How could you even *think* that you could be graced with a woman such as I? Do you not realize what I am? Your pathetic crew did nothing but feed me and give me the souls I need for my master! Now give me your soul, little boy and I promise I will make your death quick,' she hissed at me, her fangs bared and dripping with blood…my blood.

I jumped from her bed, not even bothering to get dressed and ran away, crying not only in anguish, but also in fear. Though my legs collapsed out from under me numerous times, weakened by the lack of blood in my body, I ran as fast as I could. She followed me, clawing my back and licking the blood that spilled from the incisions her knife-like talons made. Darkness began to envelop me as I slipped away. I knew that I had to make a final stand against her or die. Though I knew what I was to become, I had no desire to die.

I always carried a small dagger, a gift from the Captain of the ship when I saved his life once, in my boot and so far it had brought me great luck on my adventure. For some reason when I undressed for her I put that dagger on the bedside table. It was the only possession I snatched up to take with me when I left her bed. With the last of my strength I ripped the sheath off of it and whirled on her, stabbing her in the heart…*such as she had done to me only moments earlier.* I will never forget the look in her eyes as she died. It was a look of total disbelief. I had done what no one else had been able to do simply because, even with all her strength, she had underestimated me.

'How could *you* have defeated *me*? How could such a useless mortal possess the will or the strength to destroy my beautifully wicked soul?' she whispered before disintegrating to dust. I collapsed to the ground. That was the last thing I remembered, the world turning black as I hit.

I woke up, days later, in the cottage of a kindly old couple that had nursed me back to health. Their son found me on his way to the market the next morning after my death, or undeath, I should say. I had no heartbeat, though they fought to save me, and soon I was healthy. I did not, nor would I have told them that it was not their vigilant and tireless aid that saved me, but my new existence that made me well.

FALLEN   VAN SCOYOC

Had I known that my life was going to become something out of a nightmare, something that was truly a curse upon one's soul, I would have allowed *her* to kill me. The human will to live is a strong spirit and I simply could not allow myself to die…though many times since that night I have regretted that decision. *I have wished so many times that I had died* but all the wishing and praying in the world cannot change the fact that by human standards, I am immortal. I have even tried to take my own life, but ultimately could not bring myself to do it. I am not sure why, as I am damned either way, either by having no soul, or by ending my own life, but still I could not do it. *I have truly become one of the damned.*

My bloodlust started soon after the couple saved me. I fled their home before I could do them harm -- I would not have been able to live with myself had I hurt them after they saved me. Killing and drinking the blood of others to live, as I did when I was first turned, was bad enough…someone who helped a complete stranger, no matter what I am and have to do to exist, deserved better. I hated killing and still do. I spent many nights all those years ago in hysterical lamentations for what I had done to so many innocent people. However what I did do for the couple was return one evening while they slept, leaving them a purse full of gold coins and a note of thanks at their front door as a token of my gratitude. I never saw them again, nor did I wish to. I could not bear to face them, for surely they would have suffered a fate worse than death at my hands.

For many years now I have loathed what I am but have learned to accept it and move forward. I blame no one for what I am. My naiveté and nothing more, not even *her*, led me to this life. All of life's most important lessons are learned the hard way, and oftentimes are painful or even too much to bear. The lesson I learned has been both. I *have* learned but at the expense of my life and soul. In retrospect such knowledge does nothing to help me now but I have learned to make the most of what I am. The fact that living forever gives me many opportunities to do things that I would not have had the chance to do otherwise has been rewarding and I am grateful for those I have helped."

Farayne sat in rapt attention. How very sad for Garrison. Why would someone take advantage of such a kind young man? The woman from his story, with her haughty and superior attitude almost reminded her of her former peers. Death was too good for her…

Farayne saw that her love was staring curiously at her. She realized that she was frowning. She smiled.

"I am very sorry for what you have endured, my sweet. Life can be so unfair at times and what happened to you was wrong. May I ask you a question or do you prefer me to wait until you have finished your story?"

Garrison smiled. He was appreciative of Farayne's kind and non-judgmental nature.

"You may ask now, my dear. I am happy to answer your questions."

Farayne drew a breath. "Do you still feed from humans? You spoke of drinking human blood as if it were something that you no longer do. How do you exist?"

Garrison shrugged.

"Yes and no; to your question. At first I fed off of anyone who happened across my path when I was hungry and regretted every death I caused. I still do. I buried each of my victims and said a prayer for them…not that God would listen to anything *I* had to say, but for their sakes I hoped that He would. All that changed as I walked the countryside one evening, simply wandering as I often did, pondering forever. I came across a town stricken with some form of plague. Everyone was sick it seemed and those that were still healthy had more than their share of burden in caring for the dying. It was there that I saw an opportunity to help -- although to anyone not acquainted with what I am would hardly see my intervention as help I'm certain, choosing rather to condemn me than laud me. I began feeding on the sick and dying. I killed many, but only as acts of mercy. I could not bear to see suffering of any kind, and killed anyone who asked me to. In this time, I drink only the blood of animals. The thought makes me very sad, as I love animals so much, but I cannot bear the thought of aiding another human to their death, no matter how noble that act can be."

Farayne nodded in empathy. She did understand, much as Garrison might not think she could; she finally understood him. His

88

aloofness, his seemingly self-absorbed attitude, his cold and almost emotionless demeanor…he carried far too much pain to be happy and she knew that he might never be. Oftentimes things happened to mortals that were more than *they* could bear, why should the immortal be any different? Many times *one* lifetime proved to be too painful for a person. What could centuries do? Why should their burdens be considered anything less than unbearable? She knew that feeling herself and all too well from when her mother died. She had to be brave for far too long as her mother fought to live. When the doctor came out of her room, closing the stately oak doors as if closing off her life for good, and then gave the news to her and her father, she went numb. Her life stopped and the cold fluid of a reality she was ill prepared for congealed under her scalp, freezing her with anguish and consuming her in anger all at the same time.

Garrison once again looked at Farayne curiously. Could she tell what he was thinking?

He was lonely and had been for quite some time. He had been so apathetic in his attitude toward his beautiful guest because he had not been with a woman since those long ago nights with Isabella. He could not do to anyone what had been done to him and he was, to a degree, still ashamed of what he was. Could he ever trust a human being enough to allow them into his world? He did wish for *someone* to share his life with and he hoped that woman could be Farayne.

But she was a child…a spoiled and pampered child, much like he himself had once been. Was she adult enough to accept him, *truly* accept him for what he was or was he simply a flight of fancy for her; a new and interesting conquest that she could and probably would tire of when the mystery and intrigue of what he really was, wore off?

Should he try to make a life with her? Should he try to love again? *Forever* was far too long to be alone and so there was only one way to find out if this woman would be worthy of his love. What did he have to lose? He looked at her carefully.

"So now you know what I am, my sweet Farayne."

Farayne's bottom lip trembled and then she burst into tears.

Garrison took the sobbing girl in his powerful arms and held her as she wept and confessed her love for him. She no longer held back. The tears, the worry in her voice, the words that seemed to tumble out of her mouth faster than she could control them as she spoke of her fear of rejection. She sobbed her willingness to have him in her life no matter how. She was ready even to simply be his friend if necessary. She assured him that *nothing* would sway her feelings for him. She was surprised that she had summoned the courage to tell him that she loved him but knew that if she did not make her feelings obvious he may never know. She had nothing to lose and everything to gain if he would simply have her.

Garrison dropped his eyes.

"You say that *nothing* can change your love for me, but can you possibly love a creature such as I?"

Farayne paused only a moment before she answered.

"Oh, my sweet…I am so sorry, my beautiful, beautiful, Garrison. I ache for you and all the hurt you have endured. I love you even more intensely now that I know what you are. I thought that I could love you no more than I do, but I do love you more -- *so much more*. You are kind, caring, selfless, and humble. I could not find such traits in any mortal man, even if I searched the world over. I do love you and will *always* love you even if you can never find it in your heart to love *me*."

Garrison squeezed the sobbing girl even tighter. Never could he have expected to hear such a revelation from this dear sweet child. How could he not accept her affection? How could he *not* wish to be the lover that she wanted him to be?

He looked into her deep green eyes and found himself nearly lost in them as he pressed his cold lips gently to hers. His kiss was slow and tender, his passion evident as the kiss intensified. He wanted her, more so than he had ever wanted anything in his life, and he knew that she wanted him. He was apprehensive…not of loving her, but of hurting her.

"Farayne…I have wished to be with you…as your lover…your friend…and husband since that first night we met, but I am afraid."

Farayne started to speak once again to reassure her savior that she had wanted nothing more than the same, but a slender, cold finger silenced her.

90

FALLEN   VAN SCOYOC

"No...please, let me speak. I have been fearful of telling you how I really feel about you, hence my aloof and oftentimes indifferent behavior during our times alone. I am so afraid that you are in love with a dream, a fairytale type of man and I am not he. What if you tire of never seeing the sun rise again? What if you wish to swim in the beautiful lakes here, pick flowers or even visit the market? Oh do not get me wrong...you are more than welcome to spend as much time in the daylight as you please, my sweet, but I will not be with you when you do. I cannot. There are so many things that I took for granted while I was still mortal and now they are gone forever. I miss the sunlight on my face; I miss the early morning's crisp and fog-saturated air as the sun lifts itself to prominence in the sky. I miss...so much of it all. You must understand my love that I can *never, ever* experience any of that with you. Not at *any* point. Are you certain that you wish to spend your daylight hours alone, while I sleep in a cold and dank room?" Tears spilled down Farayne's face as she nodded emphatically.

"I love *you* Garrison...not some dream of what I think you are, for I make no presumptions. *You* are a true gentleman, as real a man as I could ever wish to meet. I wish to be with you and *only you*, my sweet, and I will make *any* sacrifices that I must, in order to do so. What is the sunlight when I can spend the rest of my life *truly* happy?"

A single tear ran down Garrison's cheek and he nearly crushed Farayne again as he held her.

CHAPTER SIX
PURE LOVE

Garrison lowered the beautiful young woman slowly onto his bed as he gingerly removed her clothing. Farayne allowed her love to undress her. Never had a man shown such care as Garrison was taking with her, and she relished every move he made. First he removed her slippers from her tiny feet, then slowly rolled her tights down her pale legs, and then unbuttoned the underslip that held her firm breasts gently in place. His hands visibly shook and Farayne smiled inwardly. How she had waited for this moment and yearned to know what his love would be like.

He pulled her slip from her and then pulled his shirt over his head. Farayne marveled at his pale and smooth chest. He was hairless, his chest muscles lean and taut…he was beautiful. He looked carefully at her, as if seeking her approval before he went any further, his ebon hair tumbling past his shoulders and onto his chest. She smiled. He smiled in return, satisfied with her answer and stood silently, sliding his pants down his legs, and climbed on top of her, straddling her curvy body. He looked at his rapturous, pure angel, naked before him in her most humble form and he felt himself stir. She was truly beautiful. Her milky white shoulders, her pert breasts and tiny nipples, her smooth stomach and the small patch of black hair that covered her undiscovered region. He moved to one side of her, sliding his hand between her legs, caressing them gently before he parted them.

"Be gentle, my sweet. I have…never…"

"I would never harm you, my love. In all my searching I have never found anything more pure than you. You are all I could ever ask for. I will love you eternally and hurting you will never happen."

He climbed back onto her, holding himself above her and parting her legs further with his own settled gingerly between them. He looked into her eyes one last time and then kissed her hungrily, passionately searching her mouth. Her kiss was clumsy but she returned the ardor he felt growing inside him. He finished the kiss, nibbling his way down her neck and to her small but firm breasts. He rubbed his cold cheek on one, then the other and felt his love shiver. He smiled as her nipples hardened to bright red points and cupping her left breast in his pale hand, gently flicked the nipple of her right breast with his tongue. She jerked and cried out as he slid his lips around the inviting gift, tugging gently. Farayne's cries of unrestrained bliss made Garrison's thighs quiver and he felt a stark and strong stinging deep in his groin that he'd thought long dead. He grasped his throbbing organ in one hand and making certain that he would not put his weight on her, slid deeply but gently into her. She cried out, arching in pain and he quickly withdrew. She begged him to enter her again and wrapped her legs around his thin sides, pulling him down to her. He lay softly on her, kissing her gently and entered her again, his mouth on hers, stifling her cries. His thrusts were smooth and soon her whimpers of pain became gasps of pleasure.

Time seemed to stop for the once spoiled socialite as her lover rocked her gently. She had no idea how long their lovemaking had lasted but she savored every second of her handsome suitor's thrusts. Farayne arched as the orgasm tore through her and cried out loudly as she came. Her ecstasy excited her savior and he wrapped his hands underneath her shoulders, pulling her into him as he pounded her roughly. Tears slid down the sides of her face and into her dark hairline, but she quickly wiped them away. If he saw her crying would he stop? She wouldn't take that chance.

She felt him shudder violently and when he came she felt it deeply inside her.

He came hard, slamming himself between her bruised thighs, moaning loudly as he emptied himself into her. The nectar that filled her was cold. Why wouldn't it be cold? He was dead. She had never paid much attention before, but now realized that every time she had touched him, he had been cold, so deathly cold. Garrison choked and convulsed one last time, then lay, exhausted on top of her, his arms trembling violently as he attempted to keep his weight from crushing her. Farayne stroked him gently, cradling him as best she could.

"I am certain that I hurt you my darling, please allow me to look."

Farayne had nothing left to hide from her lover and she felt no embarrassment at him seeing her most private garden. She nodded as a tear spilled down her cheek. She could see his blood saturated, dark nether mane as he stood, and she swallowed in fear. How badly was she bleeding? Garrison gently parted his lover's bruised thighs and she felt fingers gently probing her hidden area. She lifted her head and Garrison's lips were pursed.

"I am sorry, my sweet, I have hurt you, badly. Please allow me to clean you?"

Farayne nodded.

"Do not move. I will get a bowl of water and a cloth."

Farayne shivered in the night air and as if reading her thoughts, Garrison pulled the covers over her, gently kissing her forehead.

She closed her eyes, a smile frozen onto her smooth lips and had almost drifted off to dream when her love returned, clean water and a soft cloth in his hands.

Garrison knew that he would have to burn the stained bed sheets but he didn't care. The sheets were merely things -- a possession. His angel's comfort was more important to him than an article of bed clothing.

Farayne bit her lip as her love pressed the wet cloth to her. His strokes were tender and slow, but she still hurt. She lifted her head again and Garrison stopped, setting the cloth and bowl down. Had she angered him? Did he take her curiosity as an insult...that she possibly thought him incapable of doing a good enough job taking care of her? Garrison stood and walking to the head of the bed, took another pillow and gently lifting his queen's head to him, placed it under her head. He held her, kissing the bridge of her nose softly and nuzzling her.

"You are curious my sweet...I find that amusing. You are injured, yet you wish to see what I am doing. The extra pillow should help you see better and keep your neck from hurting as you watch."

Garrison smirked and Farayne stroked his bare chest in answer. He shivered and with a final kiss to her soft lips, he laid her gently back down and returned to his position between her legs. Farayne intently watched her lover. He was so careful with her, so tender. Then she saw it as the blood soaked cloth caught the faint

94

moonlight that spilled into the room…the gleam in his eyes as he thoroughly cleansed her. She suddenly felt very guilty. How could she have allowed him to clean her knowing what her blood, *her human blood*, which he did not drink any longer, was an unfair temptation?

"My love…please…partake of me…take as much of my blood as you wish. I am sorry that I did not think to offer myself to you sooner. If you desire my blood, whether to feed your hunger or simply because you wish it, please…"

Once again Farayne caught the look in his eyes. It was one of longing, uncertainty and Garrison licked his lips as he looked at her bloody bounty before him. Though he had not tasted human blood in many, many years he accepted her offer. With a nod he pulled her closer to the edge of the bed, slowly parting the dark hair that covered his need. She rested her legs on his shoulders and closed her eyes. She was very sore but pain did not concern her. Nothing concerned her but showing her love the same care and desire he had shown for her. She was very swollen, but he was gentle as he licked her. He was thorough and she felt the tip of his tongue as it searched her. She cried out and pulled his mouth closer to her injured cave as his tongue aroused her all over again.
His licks became deeper and more insistent as he parted her bloody lips, tasting and nibbling her, his moans of content making her light-headed.

Farayne screamed her lover's name and Garrison felt the surge as she came for the second time that night. He devoured her hungrily, the blood and her sweet juices causing him to shudder with pleasure. He partook of what her body offered him until she was completely clean. With one final kiss to her swollen, hidden lips, he removed her legs from his shoulders.

"I am going to draw us a bath my sweet. I want you to stay here while I fetch water. I keep water heating in the fireplace all the time in case I need it. While I am preparing the water, I wish you to rest."

Farayne was tired but smiled in answer and closed her eyes.

She stirred.

"Gar…"

"Hush my beautiful Farayne. I have the water ready and I will bathe us."

Farayne felt as if she were floating as her strong lover whisked her from the bed, carrying her to the awaiting bath. She was still very sore and drifted off to sleep again. She jerked what seemed like only seconds later, waking from the light sleep her body had allowed her, as her lover set her gently in the warm water. With virtually no sound, he climbed in behind her, pulling her back to lie on him in the steam.

"Is the water warm enough for you?"

Farayne nodded.

"It is perfect, my sweet."

She sighed in complete content and drifted peacefully off to a deep sleep, satisfied in a way in which she never dreamed possible. She knew that Garrison was the man of her dreams, the man she had sought for so long. How could she not be at peace? Before her dreams swallowed her in complete bliss she heard words, as if shouted back to her, being carried airily on the wind.

"I love you, Farayne. I will love you for always."

Garrison put his face in his love's hair and wept for joy.

Farayne packed her clothing quickly. Her father was at yet another gala, one where he was the guest of honor. How perfect for him. Like so many of his peers, men of import, he never tired of hearing others tell him what a wonderful man he was and how much everyone needed him.

Farayne smiled. Garrison was outside waiting for her, quieting their horses. Her horse, a black and white spotted beauty which she named Moon Maiden in honor of Aggie's brave steed, was a pleasant surprise as her lover led her, blindfolded, to the back of his manor where she stood munching hay right alongside his own horse, Hammersley. Farayne had learned to ride, something she feared that she would never do and Garrison was only too proud to buy her a horse of her own.

Farayne packed the last of her necessities and then looked at her dresser. The letter to her father seemed to almost accuse her as she stared at it. She had penned the letter from the heart but she was not weak in her assertion of freedom from court life. She *had* to leave, she *would* leave and nothing he could do would change her mind, nor any amount of men he could -- and he probably would -- send after her would maker her return to her home.

Farayne continued to eye the letter. Her bright red seal at the bottom, a gift from her mother, beckoned her to come closer. She wished to walk over to the dresser and pick up the letter, to put it in her father's bedroom but her feet would not move. Feelings of visiting the Dancing Dragon on that very first night flooded her and she closed her eyes, balling her tiny fists into clenched determination. She opened her eyes, set them on the letter and marched over to the dresser, snatching it up and holding it aloft in victory. "Nothing will stop me from seeing my life's path come to fruition…not you father nor the sway you have held over me for all these years."

Farayne went back to her bed, picked up the bag, and looked around her bedroom one last time. She would never see this place again and leaving held mixed emotions for her. While she would miss her *room*, it had been the only place she'd ever felt comfortable while in her father's house, she would not miss the terrible memories her home had often held for her. A single tear slid down her cheek and she wiped it away, then hurried quickly to her bedroom door, opening it quietly. She had to make certain that none of the maids would see her leave. Holding her bag, the same one that had belonged to her mother, in her small hands she quietly walked down the hallway, down the small flight of stairs to the second floor landing and to her father's bedroom, which sat at a strange angle from the stairs. Farayne had always liked the angle of her father's room and had wondered each time she saw it why he'd had it built that way. The room almost looked as if it had been built in afterthought. She tried the door, her hands shaking and her palms sweaty, despite the chill that had descended upon the house with the setting of the sun. It was locked. Of course it was locked! Why would it not be? Her father trusted no one and he had never trusted the servants, even after handpicking all of them! Why would she have ever thought that the door would be left open? She looked anxiously around and bit her bottom lip as she often did while she thought. Then she saw light coming from underneath the door. Her father was gone and he would *not* leave a candle burning in his room while he was not home. The light was too faint to be anything other than moonlight, finding it's way to her courtesy of the giant windows that made up one whole wall of his room. She could slip the letter under the door and he would see it when he returned! He always went to his study first and she had thought of putting the letter in there. But the servants were always in there cleaning up and dusting and if they saw her letter they might try to stop her from leaving. Farayne squatted down and slid the letter under the door, standing quickly back up and all but running to the stairwell. With a gulp of breath for courage she descended the stairs. She negotiated the steps with care and made it to the kitchen, where she held her breath as she pressed herself up against the wall across from the door that led to her freedom. The kitchen help was always a busy lot and they came and went, walked the hallways outside the kitchen and were always up to something. If anyone would catch her trying to leave, it would be them. Though most of them were dullards to the highest degree of stupidity, they were not *totally* simple-minded and her with a bag, her father out of the house…they just might figure out her plan.

She had thought and thought, giving herself headaches about the repercussions of abandoning her father and yet she came to the same conclusion each time she thought it over. Her home and court life held nothing for her and she had no reason to stay.

98

FALLEN   VAN SCOYOC

She had pledged her love to Garrison and it was with him that she would remain until the end of her life. She knew that she would never regret her decision. Though she would miss her father, she would not miss his meddling and she certainly would *not* miss life at court.

The kitchen help all seemed to disappear at the same time and so Farayne took the opportunity to run out the door, closing it behind her, running as fast as her legs would carry her to Garrison and the horses.

When she reached him she was out of breath, but smiling. Garrison looked at her curiously and then smiled uneasily. For the first time since she met him he seemed unsure of himself. "For a moment I thought that maybe you had changed your mind." Farayne stood on her toes and Garrison leaned in closer to her. "Never my love…I wish only to be with you."

They kissed and Farayne felt as if happiness had consumed her in warmth and light. She was dizzy with excitement, giddy with love and she knew that though times would not always be perfect between she and her love, he could and would offer her more than her father ever would have.

They ran to the horses and Garrison all but threw his love onto the back of her horse. She felt herself lifted and deposited in the saddle with the effortless strength her lover possessed. She looked up and as if he had flown onto his back, Garrison sat proudly on Hammersley's back. With a quick spur of his horse, he took off at a gallop and Farayne followed.

Time seemed to hold no meaning for the once socialite beauty. The days and nights passed into one and if happiness were a tangible possession that one could actually reach out and take hold of, she had happiness with both hands. Their time together was the best of her young life, but she wanted more. With each passing day, month and into the year that followed with Garrison, her mortality beckoned. She knew that if she still associated with her former peers, they would think her morbid for fixating on an event that more than likely would not happen for many years down the long road of her life. She had no worries of what anyone would think now and so she set about the task of getting what she wanted…what she *needed* if she wished to spend her life with an immortal.

Garrison would live forever and unless he brought her across, she would not; she would die. She would wither, she would fade and she would eventually crumble to dust with mortality's bane. How could she look at him -- lean, beautiful and perfect -- as her own body grew old and frail? How could she gaze at his handsome face when her eyes betrayed her in dimness? How would he run his fingers through her hair when it had all but completely fallen out? *How* could he wish to stay with her when the blossoms of her youthful beauty had fallen to decrepit rot? She could not and *would not* expect him to stay with her. How selfish could she be to even entertain the idea that he would stay with her? There was only one answer to her perplexing dilemma and she would do whatever necessary to secure an answer in the positive from her soulless lover. Her twenty-first birthday was approaching. If she began pleading with him now, *maybe* he would delight her with a yes.

Farayne sat up from her sleep with Garrison. But she hadn't slept at all. Her thoughts were much too occupied with what she wanted. While she wasn't sure how to go about asking her love for an eternity with him, she knew that it had to be done. She had decided before ever rising that one of their customary, nightly walks would be perfect to gain her savior's agreement. Why not their impending walk with the coming darkness after he woke? Farayne looked out at the setting sun as it struggled to gain her attention in its colorful end-of-day death, and smiled.

She lied back down and snuggled into her lover, enjoying the thoughts that danced in her head.

Garrison's eyes snapped open and he gazed over at his queen, his only reason for existence lying beside him.

"Hello my love," he whispered.

"Hello my king," she whispered in return.

"Shall we walk?"

"Oh yes my dear king...we shall."

The two lovers donned capes and lanterns, the lanterns more for Farayne's sake than Garrison's, as his superb night vision missed nothing, and set off on their nightly journey across the countryside. The bright light of the moon illuminated their path and all seemed at peace in their corner of the world.

Farayne held tightly to Garrison's arm and snuggled into him as the chill evening air bit into her flawless skin.

"My sweet...you know that my birthday is approaching do you not?"

Garrison squeezed his arm around her and kissed her raven head.

"Indeed I do, my love. I must confess that while I have thought and wondered, dreamed and worried, I do not have any idea of what to get you. If you can give me an idea of what your heart's desire might be, I will do my best to seek it out for you." Farayne smiled broadly. She could not have asked for a better set-up to tell her love what she wished if she had orchestrated it with the Fates themselves!

She tried to calm her thundering heart as it thudded in her chest. "My heart has but one desire my darling and one desire alone. I wish to be with you...*for eternity.*"

If Garrison's blood were not already run cold, it would have become so at that moment. He knew exactly what it was that his love requested, but how could he oblige? *Why* would he do something like that to her and *how* could she ask him to do such? Did she not fully comprehend his story? *Why* would someone intentionally wish to be vampyre? She had to know that he did not want to damn her...*she had to!*

Garrison feigned naiveté and prayed that she would not ask again. Would she be so bold as to come right out and ask if he did not grant her wish? He knew the answer to that question before it had even settled into his mind, but he had to nonetheless hope that she would not.

Putting on his best act, he answered her as calmly as possible.

"My dear, I have already told you that I will love you forever. Have I not made my intentions and my devotion to you clear enough? What more must I do to prove that you are my light, my love and my angel, for always?"

He knew the question was loaded, and not in his favor, before he even finished speaking it, but it was too late. He had asked and she would answer. How could he have been so careless with his words?

Farayne stopped walking and Garrison looked deeply into her eyes silently pleading her not to request *that* of him.

"What more must you do to prove your love for me, my sweet? I think you know the answer to that. You are clever, my dear, but I know that you are not the naïve young sailor, traveling the world with eager eyes, as you once were. I beg of you...make me yours, to walk with you in shadow and shade, to hold you during the night and hide from the sun. I will be your queen, your lover, your wife and you will be my king and my only light in a life of darkness...for all eternity."

Garrison was dubious. The trap he'd unwittingly set for himself that night out in the countryside as he and his queen walked the shadows -- that same night that he all but handed his love the damnation she wished -- played over and over in his mind. He could understand her yearning to be with him for eternity as he ached for it himself, but he was adamantly against condemning her. It had taken *all* of Farayne's persuasiveness to convince him to grant her that one and only birthday wish and he still lamented his weakness in acquiescing.

He offered her a bigger home, new clothes, jewels and his undying love, no matter how she looked as she aged...sworn on a blood oath if she desired, in exchange for retracting her wish. She refused and Garrison had not been surprised. Materially, what could he give her that she had not already owned? She was petty nobility and had grown up with the finest of everything! The guilt he felt for the one thing that, had she not met him, she would have never even considered, was overwhelming -- but it was too late. But she *had* met him; she had fallen in love with him and he with her. He had even thought of fleeing if the opportunity presented itself, fleeing and never looking back if it meant saving her from eternal hell, but he knew that he could not do that to her. He simply could not. His love for her was greater than his desire to save her from herself. She would not take "no" for an answer, he knew it and he would have to accept it.

He wanted to spend eternity with her, but hated the thought of taking her soul and forcing her to live in the abyss in which he was destined to exist. As he knew he would eventually be forced to do, he relented, albeit begrudgingly, to his queen's desire and gave her the gift of eternal life.

The morning of his love's birthday arrived and Garrison awoke from a troubled sleep. Though he could not rise to be with her, he knew that Farayne was already enjoying her final day as a mortal. She had told him her entire plan for the last day of her *life*.

"My love, I am going to rise with the dawn. I love the first rays of the sun and the feeling that the day is awakening to hasten us all on our continued journey. I wish to pick flowers and ride Moon Maiden one last time in the light. I wish to splash in the nearby stream and simply lie on the ground as the sunlight pours through the trees."

"That sounds magnificent, my sweet. You enjoy your day and I will be with you with the rising of the moon."

Smiling with an ease he did not feel, he slipped into their bedroom and awaited the next day...a day that he would loathe and love for the remainder of eternity.

Now that day had arrived...and he could feel the dread permeating every fiber of his being. For the first time ever he dreaded the setting of the sun. He knew what he had promised would come to pass and he knew that there would be no turning back. Tears spilled down his cheeks and then he openly wept, thankful that his love was nowhere around to hear him cry.

Farayne reposed in the soft grass looking up through the light filtering through the trees. It was almost magical the way the rays dotted the ground and warmed her face.

"Oh I will miss this...I will miss it all. But given the chance at eternity with Garrison, I choose my love. The only real change to my life will be the lack of sunlight, but I will gain so much more...*so much more.*"

Farayne smiled again and scooped up a handful of petals from the ground beside her. She had indeed spent the entire morning picking flowers, her baskets overflowing around her with fragrant blossoms. Moon Maiden stood grazing nearby with a flower wreath on her head and a necklace of rose blossoms. Farayne glanced over at her elegant steed and with a "whee" in childlike amusement she threw the flowers into the air. She watched them sail into the beams of light as if teasing them and giggled as they landed atop her. She would enjoy this day -- and remember it for always.

Exhausted and resigned, Garrison fell back into a fitful sleep. He hoped his love would enjoy the daylight and that the night would come and go quickly. He wished to fulfill his obligation and start anew. He'd cried his tears, rationalized his conscience and he was ready. He would have to be.

"Garrison! Garrison my love!"

The beautiful vampyre man heard his angel's melodious voice before he ever felt her alight beside him. She stroked his head, kissed his pale lips and caressed his chest.

"It is time to celebrate my birthday, my king."

Garrison slowly opened his eyes and smiled. He looked at the only window in the room and through the gaps in the heavy covering over it he could see stars. His eyes then rested on his queen, a beautiful flower wreath in her hair and flowers adorning her dress. She was a vision.

Farayne glanced upwards and touched the wreath.

"Do you like it, my love? I made one for Aggie too."

"I do my darling, I do very much. Shall we go get Aggie now?"

"Do you know where she lives?"

"I do."

Farayne smiled in mischievous delight at her love.

"Then we shall go now, my sweet."

Farayne murmured in satisfied delight, as the two lovers lie naked in each other's arms after her turning. Her crossing was the perfect end to this chapter of her life. In human years she was twenty-one years old and in the vampyre realm, she would be forever 21.

Her party had been beautiful and Aggie had stayed as late as her tired and worn down body would allow. She loved her wreath, and swore that it would always have a place of prominence on her head.

She smoked her pipe, burned fragrant herbs in the hearth and even brought a flute to play that had belonged to her late husband. Her breath came in heaving gasps as she struggled with the ancient instrument but she played as best she could and both of her new friends cheered her on with each wavering note.

The night seemed to race by much too quickly and with each passing minute, Garrison could feel the heavy burden in his heart threatening to consume him. But he put on a brave face for Farayne...and for Aggie.

With hugs and kisses to her friends, she'd returned to her home as the flames in the couple's hearth ebbed to smoldering embers. Had the night not been so damp and cool the party would have been held outside, but Farayne feared for Aggie's health should she catch a chill. Aggie protested an inside party when the best way to appreciate the Master was under His moon and stars, but Farayne had been adamant.

Aggie was grateful for her dear friend's concern. She knew that in the advanced stages of her life such kinship and merriment did not come along very often. How she too would treasure her dear Lady Gleneden's birthday.

Farayne smiled lovingly at her king. He was selfless and accommodating. She was not blind. She knew that he did not wish to turn her and she would forever be grateful for his devotion and willingness to compromise his honor for her. Their lovemaking had been rapturous, his animalistic thrusts not at all painful, and as she screamed his name in ecstasy, he bit deeply into her neck. She continued gyrating against him as he slammed his exploding shaft deeply into her. His normally strong voice was nothing more than a whimper of ecstasy as his nectar spread deeply into her awaiting coffer. He felt the contractions of her viselike tunnel and with each constriction, he thrust a bit more as he fulfilled her request -- his mouth locked on her neck.

He released her neck and kissed her passionately. She eagerly accepted the blood -- her own blood on his lips -- to her mouth as she returned the kiss with a passion that made him whimper again. He had nearly forgotten that such fervent desire could exist. It was as if all the love she felt for him could be delivered in such a small and simple gesture.

He lay down beside her and watched her. She was weak, very weak and he slid his hand between her pale breasts to feel her heartbeat. It was there, but very faint. He slid his arms underneath her, cradling her softly. A tear made its way haltingly down his cheek. His love, his eternal treasure lay in his arms pale, bleeding, and gazing at him as if he were a god, though he felt more devil at that moment than savior. She stroked his face gingerly and he kissed her hand.

"Now you must drink from me, my sweet to complete the crossing."

She nodded slowly.

Garrison bit deeply into his own wrist and pressed it to her mouth.

"Here, my angel, partake of me, of *my* offering and be mine…for always."

Farayne turned her head and sat up as the blood dripped onto her face.

"Farayne, you must drink."

She smiled.

"I know that my king…but I do not wish to drink from your wrist. There is another part of you I wish to drink from."

Garrison's eyebrows scrunched in question and he followed his lover's eyes down to his lower body swathed between the soft bedcovers. He shook his head.

"No, my love. I cannot…I *will not* disrespect you by doing that. That is something that I have seen the whores in back alleys do, and you are not of such low ilk."

Farayne smiled. Garrison was so caring, so gentlemanly…it truly amazed her. Many of the young men she'd known tried to convince her to enjoy their organ and she'd refused. Why would she want to do anything like that…for *them*? What had *they* done for *her* that would make her wish to do something so immensely personal for them? They were not worth the time it took for them to wish her pleasure upon them. They all had felt the sting of her harshness, their egos bruised as she laughed and walked away. One man grabbed her arm in anger and pulled her back to him. A swift kick between his legs and he unhanded her immediately, his howls of pain interspersed with apologies.

"My love…this is what *I* want. You will not be disrespecting me in *any* way by allowing *me* to pleasure *you*. Please…finish my birthday off with one last gift?"

Garrison bit his bottom lip and shook his head, his eyes downcast.

"How can I reconcile myself to allow such a thing when my heart already holds such guilt?"

Farayne smiled.

"Maybe I can help you."

She climbed on top of her lover and straddled him, rubbing her wetness against him as she kissed him brutally. Blood flowed freely from her neck, between her ample breasts and slithered its way down her curvy figure. He gasped and began to harden as she kissed her way down his trembling body. When she got to his throbbing rod she took it gently into her mouth, sucking softly and then deeply, pulling hard on his manhood. Garrison arched and cried out, thrusting into his queen's mouth.

"Wait…my love…wait. While I enjoy this, it will not give you what you need. On my dresser you will find a long, thin piece of smooth metal. It has many uses, as a tool and if I need it, to secure my hair when I am working. It will do the trick I believe. Bring it to me."

Farayne weakly arose from the bed and did as her lover asked, walking unsteadily to the dresser. She found the metal and paused. Garrison began to run to her thinking that she might faint from the loss of blood but she turned and with a mischievous smile, brought the slim piece of metal to him.

Garrison lied back and held his erect manhood tightly, threading the piece into his cock. He continued feeding the piece deeper and deeper, inch-by-inch until he cried out, arching in agony. A tear slid down Farayne's cheek as her lover's face contorted. It was obvious that what he'd done…for her…was painful. He'd injured himself in order to fulfill her request. She would make certain to please him in such a way that he would never regret

108

allowing her to drink from his shaft, but instead would come to her again and again asking her to please him.

He squeezed his member and blood spurted from the tip.

"Now my love," he gasped, "now you may have what you need."

Farayne wasted no time in lowering her head and taking her lover's bleeding organ deeply into her mouth. She gagged at first, but refused to stop, sucking like a starving babe, deeply, gently, hard and then soft as the nourishment she needed slid down her throat.

Garrison began crying out louder and louder as his pain was forgotten, replaced with rapture like he'd never before felt. The harder his lover sucked, the more he cried out. He began thrusting slowly and then rapidly as blissful desire engulfed him. He could no longer hold his passion in check and he screamed so loudly that it hurt his angel's ears as his organ erupted in unbridled orgasm like a blood and semen volcano.

Farayne simply sucked harder, pleasing her lover all the more as the nearly drowning surge flowed into her mouth. She gagged and coughed and before Garrison could ask her to stop, she had her mouth locked on his pulsing member again, sucking deeper and deeper, taking all that she could from him. Garrison lied back on the bed, winded, his smooth chest quivering and the throbbing of his manhood slowly receding as Farayne finished drinking from him.

She kissed the soft organ and climbed up her king's body, planting tiny kisses as she did. When she reached his face, she kissed him, slowly, deeply and with all the passion her tiny body contained. Garrison finished the kiss and she lied down on his chest.

"Garrison, my love...I'm cold."

"You are dying, my sweet, but when you awake I will be here waiting for you. Close your eyes and do not be frightened."

Farayne nodded and closed her eyes as she was attacked by horrible pain. She screamed and cried out, but Garrison embraced her tightly as her body contorted. Tears slid down his cheeks as he held her firmly immobile in his arms until she stopped thrashing.

"Farayne? Farayne?"

His love lay motionless and he could no longer hear or feel her heart. She was dead.

"I love you, my beautiful queen. I will see you soon."

CHAPTER SEVEN
LIFE AND DEATH IN THE VAMPYRE REALM

Garrison wiped away tears as the screaming started once again. He checked the chains and lock and backed away as his love's nails caught on his flesh, tearing his arm. She fell to the floor, licking the blood, the cold stones holding the sustenance she so desperately craved.

He stood back and watched her, like a wild beast, her hair torn and disheveled, her clothes soiled and ripped to shreds. Since her crossing he had stayed with her each day and night, sobbing and pleading to a god he did not know any longer, to spare his love the humiliation of what she was to become and what it would do to her.

"Forgive me, my love, I beg of you."

"You! Bring me blood! Bring me nourishment *now*! I need blood and yours will do as well as anyone else's! In fact, I prefer yours as I already know it!"

She laughed hysterically, her words guttural, unnatural and hurtful. Garrison stepped backward and continued staggering until he fell back against the far wall of the basement. Time seemed to stop as he sank down it slowly, his head in his hands as his lover's wicked laughter brought back painful memories of times past.

How could he have done such a thing to the woman he loved? He should have been stronger, he should have refused her request, even at the risk of losing her, but he knew that what was done, was done. He made the only woman he had truly ever loved into the animalistic spawn of evil that she had become, and he would take care of her. That was the least he could do. Each time he fed her the blood of animals he brought home from his nightly hunts, she wished to kill him. She could not actually do so as the chains in the walls held her bound, but it was not from lack of trying. She swiped at him, kicked at him and tried as hard as she could to break herself free. Maybe he should allow her to kill him? What if he could not save her? What if he could never divert her violent lust for human blood?

Garrison had already run the scenario though his mind many times of what he would do if he failed at saving his queen. Though he was patient and worked with her each night, he had to be realistic and admit to himself that sometimes there was no saving a person once they had crossed. There were some that the crossing simply did not work for…not in the way it was supposed to. Life was eternal, but so was the evil violence that came with it. If he had to bring himself to the realization that Farayne could not be saved, he would kill her, then chain himself to the basement wall and holding his lover tightly in his arms, set his manor on fire. He had enough oil to do it and it would be a final rest for them both.

"I will return in only a little while with your food, my love."

He did not enjoy hunting and with such a heavy heart he enjoyed it even less this night. He had bagged a few rabbits and hoped that they would nourish his love. It seemed as if he wandered the woods by their home aimlessly while he sought food for her, even though he knew that was not the case. He stopped in his tracks and looked up. A faint glow in the distance caught his watery eyes. It was home…a home that he nearly hated. Forcing his feet to move, he descended the hill that led to her…

He laid the dead rabbits and the bowl of blood carefully at his love's bare feet. Would she drink?

His eyes drifted up and down his queen's bone thin frame. Where she had once been curvy with a sensual figure, she was now gaunt and starved. So many times he had come to the basement, axe in hand to release her, but simply could not do so. He loved her too much to let her go. Her toe and fingernails were crusty and long and she was filthy from head to toe from the fits she often threw on the cold, hard floor. She smelled horribly.

Farayne looked the carcasses over and then snatched one up, popping the head quickly into her mouth. The rabbit's glazed eyes oozed from its head as she squeezed its neck, hard. She bit deeply into the skin, tearing it away from the skull. Garrison watched her and wiped his eyes.

She finished the rabbit and then picked up the bowl of

blood, pushing the other rabbit away from her with her foot. She downed the bowl of sustenance quickly and then licked the inside of it. With a blood stained mouth, she eyed *him* warily as she licked her lips. Garrison cringed and put his hands up in defense. Oftentimes the bowls he set at her feet were thrown at him when she finished her meal. This time no bowl came sailing at his head, only to shatter against the wall. Farayne calmly set the bowl on the floor and pushed at the other rabbit again and then pulled it over to her, biting into its back and ripping it apart.

'Thank you," came the mumbled words as his lover chewed and licked, eating the raw meat and savoring the blood that dripped down her body.

If it could have, Garrison's heart would have leapt for joy. Those two little words had been the only decent thing she had said to him in the three weeks since her crossing. He tried to maintain his composure as he spoke.

"You are very welcome, my angel."

Though Garrison knew this brief exchange was a long way from where his love needed to be, to walk openly with him and live her life to the fullest she could as a vampyre, it was at least a step in the right direction.

Each day the newest member of the vampyre realm accomplished a little more until she was drinking animal blood regularly.

Garrison wept for joy the day she took her final step.

He slowly walked down to the basement the customary bowl of nourishment in his hand. He set the food down in front of her and stepped back. Farayne sniffed the bowl, and then picked it up.

She looked up at her king, her eyes hollow and glazed and took a sip of the liquid. She swished it around in her mouth, almost as if tasting a fine wine. Garrison smiled and had to suppress a laugh. He was rapturous at something so trivial! At least she was willing to try and *enjoy* the blood. A few weeks earlier he would not have been so sure.

Farayne swallowed the liquid, drank the entire contents of the bowl and then reached out to her love. Garrison fell to his knees, cradling her and sobbing loudly. They had made it…they had *finally* made it.

In recognition of such a momentous event, Garrison decided to unshackle his love even though he wasn't certain he could fully trust her. He had to admit his fears -- that she would escape or do him harm -- but it was soon evident the moment that the locks fell to the floor that all his fears had been for naught. She threw herself into his arms and held him tightly.

"I love you, Farayne. I love you and I wish you to marry me…please my darling, be my wife for all eternity?"

Garrison knew that his timing could not have been worse, but his heart was about to burst with the love he felt for this tiny creature that had so deeply enchanted him. Even her awful words, the barbs she so carefully stabbed into his heart could not sway his love for her and he wished to be with her for always. Farayne burst into tears.

"*I love you, Garrison and I will…I will marry you!* You have answered every prayer I have prayed since I first met you. I was so afraid that you never could…*never would* love me the way I love and worship you. You are everything to me, my prince, and I cannot exist without you! Thank you *so* much for not giving up on me. I am *so* sorry for all the terrible things I did and said to you. Can you ever find it in your heart to forgive me? I swear I did not mean to cause you pain. It was as if I was watching something awful happen but was helpless to stop what the horrible bitch said and did to you. Please my love…*please do not send me away.*"

Garrison squeezed his angel even tighter.

"Never, my sweet. I will never leave you. I am yours…for always and cannot tell you how happy I am that you will be my bride. Would you like to bathe with me?"

Garrison knew that Farayne held cleanliness in the highest

regard and now that her right faculties had returned, she would be very upset if she could smell how horribly she stank. He felt his love nod and whisked her off her feet, still cradling her tightly. He carried her upstairs and sat her on their bed then set about preparing their bath. He carried bucket after bucket of steaming water that would relax and rejuvenate them, to the tub. For the first time he took a moment, realizing that he truly relished the mist that arose from the pool of water and the scent of the roses he generously sprinkled into it. Farayne smiled. How many men would have sprinkled fresh rose petals into bath water for the woman they loved?

Little did Farayne know that Garrison was only too happy to do so for her...*anything for her*. He never knew that something he had never given much thought to, except out of necessity, would fill him with such anticipation.

Garrison turned back to his queen, and she was standing, slowly sliding what was left of her clothing from her. He had to physically fight back the tears he knew would eventually spring from his eyes as he scanned her starved body. He decided to quickly change the subject, hoping that he could cheer himself if she were happy.

"My queen, I have a new dress for you and now that you are better, can have many more delivered here for you." Farayne squealed like a small child and clapped her hands, her bare breasts jingling. Garrison felt himself stir and unbuttoned his pants. Farayne rushed to him and pulled them down, then took his hardening manhood into her mouth.

"My angel...I am...I am not clean...please..." Garrison whispered breathlessly as Farayne's mouth rapidly tugged his organ. Garrison cried out and thrust as Farayne began pulling harder and harder. It had not been that long since he'd felt her moist mouth on him, but long enough for him to know that he never wished to be without the feeling again. Harder and harder she took him until he cried out as he filled her with his rapture. Farayne licked the errant juice from the tip of his rod and smiled.

"Now I am ready to bathe."

They bathed each other and Garrison even trimmed Farayne's unsightly toe and fingernails, then curled up in his...*their* warm bed to await the oncoming day. Though he felt badly about doing so, he wrapped her tightly in his arms as they slept, in case she tried to flee. She did not and when he awoke after sunset, she was smiling at him.

Garrison once again burst into tears and kissed his angel sweetly, passionately and squeezed her in a crushing embrace.

"How would you like to go for a walk, my sweet? There is a whole new world out there that is waiting for us to explore...*together*."

"I would like that, my love."

Much to Garrison's amusement; Farayne was like a child seeing everything for the first time. She marveled at being able to spot their own kind a they walked the town, though those she spotted were not as delighted at being seen for what they were as she was at seeing them, she delighted at being able to hear everything that was said and her sense of smell was very acute. Garrison was overjoyed that instead of languishing in the darkness of the basement, they were wandering the shadows. No one looked twice at them except in respect, human couples nodding at the seemingly royal pair as they paraded, heads held high, through the streets.

"My sweet...could we please...could we go see my dear Aggie?"

Garrison began to protest but one look into Farayne's wide, pleading eyes and he knew that he could not resist any request she made. He was powerless against her. While the thought terrified him in a way that he could not describe should Aggie fear her once human friend and lash out in that fear, he was bound to do anything for his bride-to-be. What would he do if Aggie feared

116

Farayne and refused to see her? It would break his angel's heart and he knew it. He would have to deal with that if it happened. So far the wise woman had shown no fear of *him*, but that could have been only because of Farayne being human. Garrison looked up at his love, aware that he'd had his head bowed in thought.

Garrison dreaded the trip to the old woman's house. It seemed that he spent far too much time in dread as of late, but he simply could not help himself.

Farayne knocked on the door and listened. Never before could she have heard it but this time she did…footsteps shuffling along. She smiled.

"Who be ye?"

Aggie was once again the illiterate, dirty, unkempt crone she had become accustomed to being when there were the simpletons of her peers about. It also helped to keep her safe if people had no idea what she truly was, what intelligence she possessed.

"Aggie, it is your Farayne and Garrison!"

Aggie threw the door open and Farayne embraced the crone in a loving hug. Tears streamed down Aggie's face as she held the girl tightly.

"Come in, please, both of you."

Aggie was old, but not blind and she felt the chill of death, not only as she held her young friend, but also when Garrison stepped into the room -- in a way she had never felt before. It was as if the reaper himself had slipped in to pay her a visit. Regardless, Aggie hugged Garrison and motioned for both of the youngsters (at least Farayne was a youngster compared to her!) to sit down.

"Now missy, you sit down and tell me how you both have been."

Garrison smiled at Aggie and she winked at him.

Farayne smiled uneasily and then her smile broadened.

"You may find what I have to tell you, difficult to hear and even more difficult to understand my dear friend, but you have done so much for me…I wish you to know…"

Farayne knew that she was stammering and she hated doing that, so she simply began her tale.

"Aggie…I will simply tell you…"

Aggie put up a hand.

"Then tell me outside, my girl. I wish to enjoy the night as I hear of your newest adventures." Farayne began to protest her aged friend being in the cold night air, but a steely eye from the old woman silenced her. Farayne smirked.

"As you wish, Aggie."

The trio trekked outside and Garrison helped Aggie build a fire. The old witch settled back with her pipe, the fragrant smell of herbs hanging in the air. She was ready to hear Farayne's newest tales.

Farayne did indeed not hold back, telling Aggie about her desire to join the vampyre realm to be with Garrison. Much to her delight, as they chatted in the brisk night air, the popping of the fire their only audience, Aggie loved and accepted the new Farayne, never showing fear or loathing as the former Lady had expected her to.

"I knew you had changed, my dear…I felt it and have expected it. Do you think I did not know what Garrison was the moment I first met him? I could tell that he is a noble and kind lad. I have no fear of him and I have none of you. I did not know when, but I knew this was to come. It was simply confirmed when you and my dear Garrison walked through my door. I am well acquainted with the darker ones that walk amongst us. Neither of you are of a dark spirit. While you may be of the darker realm, you do not posses the aura to be of dark heart. You are both my children and I accept you. If this young man whom you have devoted yourself to makes you happy then that is all any of us can ever hope for."

Farayne wept with joy at hearing those words, words that she never expected to hear, slide from Aggie's cracked and dry lips.

Throwing her arms exuberantly around her friend's neck she asked something that she prayed Aggie would agree to.

"Aggie…once I have become fully acclimated to this life, as I am still in the transition of …well, it is difficult to explain, but I am not ready yet to be what I am," Aggie nodded. She understood but Farayne simply continued to stumble over her words realizing how inarticulate she sounded, "once I am where I need to be in this new life, will you marry Garrison and I? He has already asked me and I have accepted."

Aggie's darkened eyes shone brightly.

"So, that explains the glow."

Farayne's eyebrows scrunched in question.

Aggie cackled happily.

"You may be of the undead, my dear child, but a woman never glows like *that* unless he has received a proposal or she is with child. I do not know if the undead can have children, so I had to assume that you managed to capture the heart of this young man and that he asked you to be his."

Farayne smiled broadly. Would she ever get used to how intuitive Aggie was? If she lived for the next two or three centuries would she ever be able to be so adept at reading people? She hoped so.

Aggie spoke and when she did, both vampyre caught a tinge of sadness in her voice.

"My sweet child, while I posses great knowledge and the ability to do many things that have been tossed aside as we travel along to more advanced times, I am not a woman of the cloth. Any marriage I perform would not be valid and certainly would not be accepted by the church."

It was Garrison that spoke this time, his deep voice breaking the night.

"We are damned, my noble lady. No clergy member would consider any ceremony conducted in our stead holy or even recognizable. If my Farayne wishes you to marry us…please…marry us in the ways of the earth. You are a wise woman…the earth is your mother and father, *your family*, and we wish to be married by a woman who realizes that not all treasures can be held in one's hand…but instead, more importantly must be carried in one's heart."

Aggie wept.

CHAPTER EIGHT
AN END AND NEWFOUND PATHWAYS

Whether by force of will, by a kind act of fate, or because of Garrison's sheer refusal to allow his angel to become the hideous animal she'd been while chained in the basement, Farayne adjusted to her new life very quickly. Garrison tested her one evening by cutting open his arm and offering it to her. He had to make certain that in case something happened to him she would not revert to wanting human blood. He could not bear the thought that she would be hunted down and murdered for doing what she had to in order to survive. She shook her head and pushed away his arm.

"No my sweet...the very thought sickens me."

Garrison squeezed her tightly and wept. Between his sobs he kissed her.

"Marry me soon, my love...please. I want to know that if I were to die that I would have lived with you as my best friend, my wife...my soul and carrying my name."

Farayne looked deeply into her lover's dark eyes and kissed him softly, wiping away his tears.

"I wish to be married under a full moon...please, my sweet."

"Anything...anyplace you desire, my love."

It did not take as long, as Garrison feared it would, and by the end of the month Farayne had adjusted to her new life. At the very first full moon, she and Garrison married. Farayne insisted on not marrying until she was secure in her new life and could make her husband the best wife possible. She wanted nothing more to do with her mortal life and if she were to marry, she wished it to be as a stable member of vampyre society. Aggie married them under a large, orange full moon in a beautiful ceremony, just as Farayne wished.

FALLEN   VAN SCOYOC

Farayne watched the sky. The morning was a grayish glow and she knew that she had little time left. It appeared as if it would be an overcast dawn. Maybe that would buy her a little while to finish reminiscing...

The years seemed to race past the happy couple, but neither paid any attention. All they ever thought of was what they could offer others who were less fortunate than them. They helped the local townsfolk when they could and made merriment wherever they went. None of their friends suspected the lovely couple to be anything other than charitable and kind folk who wished to ease the daily suffering of the many downtrodden they saw.

Aggie was a frequent visitor to the Maxwell home and they to hers. She never considered them anything but her children. They were not vampyre -- they were her children, no more, no less. Garrison wept each time Aggie called him "son." He enjoyed the pleasure it gave her in proclaiming him as her own son. He had never felt such love, not even from his parents and in turn he loved the weathered old woman as if she had birthed him.

Farayne loved her kindly witch deeply, and was inconsolable when she died only a few years after marrying the happy couple.

Aggie had never said that she was feeling poorly or that she thought the time had come for her to go on the day she died. A woman such as herself would not have. The earth birthed her and it was time for her to return to that sod. There was no need for sadness. The cycle of her life was complete and she had done, seen and accomplished more than most other women of her time. She had truly been fortunate.

"Why, my love...why would she not tell us that she felt poorly? We could have saved her, we could have done...*something!*"

Farayne screamed in anguish as she knelt at her dear witch's feet, Aggie's well-worn bible clasped firmly in her hands, a smile on her face, wrapped in her favorite shawl, with her rocking chair in front of the hearth.

"My sweet, that is not what she would have wanted and you know that. She did not wish you to be upset, not any more so than you are now. *You know how I tried to convince her to join us and she would not.* Do you not think it would have broken her heart to see you imploring for her to make a choice that she was not going to make?"

Even though Garrison could speak the words of rationale to comfort his love, he did not feel them himself. He took Aggie's death particularly hard, blaming himself for not being able to convince her to live eternally. So many times he had offered to bring her across in payment, not only for what she had done for Farayne, but also for treating him as warmly as she had. He knew that a woman of her pure heart and stature would never take the chance of succumbing to the darkness that often took one after crossing, such as nearly happened to his love, but hoped that she would be one of the exceptions. The kind vampyres were not as plentiful as the horrid ones of their kind, but *there were* kind vampyres. Not all of them were the bloodthirsty savages they had the reputation for being. Garrison *knew* that if he were able to help Farayne he could help Aggie to stay one in the light with her Maker and her heart. He tried and tried, begged and pleaded, hoping that she would say "yes."

She never did.

"My dear boy…you know that you are my son as far as I am concerned. While I appreciate the offer…more than you could ever know, I wish to be with my beloved Kellan. My other children might miss me and they might not. I cannot be concerned with their thoughts of me and the simple way in which their father and I raised them. We did the best we could, did what we thought best for them and I think we did well. We each live our lives as we will and follow the path that seems best for us. My time on earth has been well spent and I can hear the good Lord calling me home to tend His gardens. It would be an honor to do so."

Garrison simply nodded in reply. There was no reason to try and dissuade her; her mind was made up. Her reasons were not

122

frivolous nor were they the ramblings of a woman who wished suicide. They were the clear and well thought out desires of a woman who wished to die as she lad lived…her own way.

With the last words she ever spoke to either of her 'children' she proclaimed how she would never leave the beautiful couple and that with each full moon she would be with them. At the time neither of them understood their witch's cryptic statement. She wished it that way…

The night of Aggie's burial found both vampyres sobbing hysterically. Garrison had labored with the effort of digging their dear friend's final resting place and was heartbroken. After staring at the shovel for the longest time he snatched it up in anger and began driving it into the soil. He knew that if he did not start digging and continue until the grave was dug, he would not be able to do it.

As much as he tried to remain detached to help his love through her grief, he could not. He sobbed as despondently as she did. They held each other until they collapsed to their knees and then set about the task of burying one of God's own.

The sobbing couple carefully followed Aggie's burial instructions. They were simple and fitting for the amazing woman who had shunned wealth and comfort for the rough and oftentimes hard ways of country life she'd been so happy to live.

As per her instructions, Aggie was buried naked so that she could go back to the earth from which her Father had made her. Also in accordance to her instructions, Farayne planted roses and many herbs around her grave. Aggie's reasoning was simple…that was to be done so that anyone who ever needed them could take them from her final resting place with her blessings. Farayne dug deep into her heart for a fitting and final farewell prayer for her dear friend. With the last of her strength, she said good-bye to her beloved witch, vowing never to forget her.

This incredible woman, her only true friend, had opened her eyes and saved her so many years ago from the life of boredom she'd expected to live.

Farayne had forever to remember her friend and she always would. While the earth could reclaim her body for the life giving nourishment it would give the land, she knew that Aggie's eternal soul would always be watching over them. Her eternal sleep was a well-deserved one and she was indeed tending God's garden now.

True to their word, neither of the beautiful vampyres ever forgot the amazing woman. With each full moon, they lit a candle on her grave, sitting on a thick blanket while breathing in the teasing aroma of the roses and herbs and reminisced on the impact she'd made on both their lives.

Each coming of the dawn found them both standing from their night of remembrance and just as they were about to leave, the candle would go out. The first time it happened, Farayne and Garrison both looked around and then at each other, wondering how such an occurrence could have happened. The air was still and nothing stirred to make such a gust of wind…but then they remembered Aggie's promise and it all made sense. The old witch told them both that she would be with them each full moon and as if telling them that the sun was rising and they needed to get home, it was she who blew out the candle, chasing them from the oncoming rays of daylight. They grew accustomed to her helpful warning after a while and in answer to her thoughtfulness would each intone, "Good night, Aggie…with love we will see you with the next full moon."

With Aggie gone the two vampyres traveled the world together. They always considered their quaint, country manor their home and never failed, even when out of the country, to remember their witch with each full moon. Farayne did indeed get to see the many sights she had longed to see with her love. It seemed as if all her dreams had come true.

124

The couple sailed the seas, visiting the exotic ports of the Far East, caravanned at night across the deserts, marveled at the ruins of civilizations that had been ancient, hundreds of years before either of them had ever been born, dined with important Potentates and reveled with the upper class of Paris' most elite circles.

Farayne never tired of seeing the world, of going on new adventures and embraced each night as if it were her last.

The years passed, but the couple's happiness would not continue the fairytale path as the beautiful young woman had hoped. Farayne would soon have to make one of the most heart-wrenching decisions of her life, a decision she could never have prepared for.

As they walked the countryside one evening, Garrison seemed unusually nervous. Farayne could sense that something was wrong.

"Garrison, my sweet…something troubles you and yet you have said nothing. Please talk to me."

Garrison's dark eyes pained and he stopped to sit on a large rock under a tree, the same one they often sat on when they stopped to marvel the stars or simply to enjoy the quiet of the night. Taking his love's hands in his he kissed them softly.

How could he tell her what he bore in his heart? Would his angel be able to understand what this meant for them? He'd sworn to love and protect her. He could and would love her for all the ages, but in his vow of protection he had let her down…he'd let them *both* down. She…*they both*, were in great danger and he had no idea how or when it could have happened. They'd been so careful, taken numerous, exhaustive precautions…yet none of it had mattered.

"Sit, my sweet…sit for I bear grave news that you must hear.

Farayne obeyed as Garrison fidgeted. That was never a good sign. He was not the type of man to fidget and she had seen him do it only once before…when he told her that her beloved Aggie had passed away.

"We must leave this place and never return…ever."

Farayne's eyes widened in shock.

"But…but…"

A slender finger silenced her.

"We have been discovered. I do not know how, I do not know when and at this point it does not matter. While I was in town, I overheard men of the clergy talking about the evil that had infected the countryside. They spoke of the many dark ones who roam the countryside and then spoke of a man and woman, giving our descriptions and saying that we are of the devil." Farayne was incredulous.

"But *how* could anyone have found out, my love?"

Garrison shook his black locks.

"I do not know, dearest, but we are in danger. The men that spoke of us talked of coming here and killing us both. They think we truly are demons!"

"But we are not, darling! Look at all the good we have done, all the people we have helped! How many people would have starved or been thrown out of the meager accommodations they have had it not been for us? I do not I expect us to be treated better than others, but surely if these men of the clergy knew that we are of pure heart, they would reconsider? Though we may be a part of the darker realm of life, that does not mean that we are of the darkness or that we revel in the evil that can accompany it!"

Garrison pursed his lips and once again slowly shook his head.

"They are from the local church, my dear, the church we do not ever and *have not* ever attended, yet we have made ourselves seen around town. That alone is enough to make them angry. We live here and yet do not attend services. In their eyes, that is an insult to them that we think their church is not good enough for us…or worse yet…we are simply ungodly. You know what a religious town this is. Our actions or lack thereof would raise suspicion for anyone else. Why should we be different? Why I did not think of that, what our presence in town could mean for us if anyone began paying attention sooner, I do not know. We are creatures of the undead…to those that are ignorant, we are spawns of Lucifer, or we would not be undead."

"Maybe if we talk to them, they will see that we are peaceful. It could not hurt to try could it, dearest? We go to them in peace before they come to us? If we ask that they withhold any further judgment until they have had time to get to know us, as they would anyone else in town maybe they will see that we are not what they believe us to be. I have no qualms with the church, with any church as long as they teach the true word of God and do not foist their own desires upon us! If they wish us to attend, I would not mind doing so every once in a while when we are in town."

Garrison almost had to smile. Always the optimist, his love was certain that her charms would work on the simpletons of the town.

"No, my love…it is too late for that. Had they wished to know anything of us before making a decision, they could have visited us at any time. There can be no dialogue with those of such closed-minded hate. We must leave, this night, while we still can. The man who seemed to be the leader, a Bishop I am certain of it, said that they would come tomorrow evening, as it is a holy night for many of those within the church's upper echelon. We would be their proof of a pious and devoted life against the devil if they were to parade us around in front of the townspeople and then murder us. No my love, we have no other choice."

Garrison wasted no further time trying to convince his beloved that they needed to leave. He simply took her hand in his and started home. The time it would take to convince her would be time cut off their lives and he would not allow that. He didn't care much at all what happened to him, but he would not allow the woman who had given up everything of her mortal life to be with him to suffer at the hands of religious zealots, hell-bent on destroying them for nothing more than power. He had found happiness and if he were to die that very night, he would die happy having seen all of life with his beautiful bride and known true love before eternal rest.

The hurried trip back to the manor was silent and solemn. They each felt as if they were already doomed…they were simply walking the final mile to whatever fate awaited them. Farayne had heard of those condemned to the gallows and wondered if she and Garrison's trip home was in any way what it felt like to be one of them, having to walk to their own hanging.

The entire way home Garrison looked around nervously and hurried his queen far faster than her legs were capable of carrying her. Nevertheless she pushed her thin body as she never had before. Once home Garrison seemed to feel as if they were in immense danger…more so than they had been on the journey back. That troubled Farayne. Garrison's instincts were never wrong. Their house, which once was a welcome sense of comfort for them, now seemed like a friend who had betrayed their trust.

They were no sooner packed with what little they could carry when they heard voices outside. Garrison quickly looked out the window. The angry clergy and townspeople had come a night early, he could only assume, in hopes of catching them unaware.

"Farayne? Farayne!"

Garrison tore through the house looking for his beloved wife.

"I am here, my love. Who is outside?"

"It is *them*, my angel, we must leave and *we must leave now*! We have no time to be slowed down by personal objects. Leave everything and let us go."

Garrison stole a glance through the window at the man he assumed to be the leader. It was the same man from the previous night in town when he saw them all talking. He was the one who

128

plotted their demise and he was indeed a Bishop. He held a large bible in his hands and the garment was unmistakable. Garrison could be considered damned as a member of the vampyre realm, but he had grown up in the church and he knew the garb and customs of it. Two men stood, one on each side of him, holding crosses and lanterns.

"Children of Lucifer, come out to us now! We have wiped out your cohorts and you have no place to run! You have no further legions with which to spread your evil! Atone for your servitude to the Dark One and we will end your pathetic lives as quickly as possible! We are servants of God, doing His will and for His grace! Should you choose to cleanse your soul, devoting it to Him before dying, your peace in death will be assured. If we must come into the abode of the devil to retrieve you then we will and you will feel His wrath, the wrath of the Almighty striking you down to the depths from which you were spawned! Your souls are damned, your lives useless...*repent, repent, repent!*"

The words rang in Farayne's ears like a guilty verdict announced in a crowded courtroom.

The lovers indeed took nothing with them, and never looked back at their home, as it was set ablaze, by the murdersome townsfolk, led by the clergyman screaming passages from the bible. They managed to reach the river, where Garrison kept a small boat but Farayne hardly felt safe. She had never seen this boat before, but it seemed as if her love had always been prepared for the day that they could be discovered. Garrison gently picked Farayne up and set her in the boat.

"Come my love, we must get you away."

The words hit Farayne like a club.

"Get *me* away? Darling, what of *you?*"

"There is no time, my sweet. They are right behind us. They saw us escape and will be here in moments. It matters not what happens to me, you must go and go now. *You must go on without me.*"

Garrison stopped speaking and Farayne knew that his final words were that...final. As he had done when he admitted to saving her life that first night they met, he stated what he had to say and that was it, he wished to discuss the matter no further. Farayne was not one to simply leave someone she loved behind and certainly not her husband...her only reason for existence. She was little more than shadow without him.

"I will not! We live together we die together. I have no use for a life without you my love!" Farayne tried desperately to climb out of the boat, but Garrison pushed her back in.

"I will not leave without you, my king!"

Garrison's eyes flashed but his voice was not unkind.

"You *must* leave me, and you *will*. Always know that the years I have spent with you have been the happiest of my existence. If I must die now, know that it is with a happy heart that I go to my death. I will accept this eternal sleep and take with me the knowledge that I have known true love and true love has known me. Never forget me, my queen."

With a quick kiss to his wife's pale lips, Garrison pushed the boat away from the shore. As he stood watching his love, his life, float away from him, a single tear ran down his cheek. Farayne sobbed hysterically as she saw the men come charging over the hill to the dock. Garrison raised his hand in a solemn salute and in a moment it was jerked down and pinned behind him by the Bishop. She was helpless as Garrison stood there, allowing the men to surround him, ripping and tearing at him as a pack of wild dogs would a wounded sheep. A pitchfork was raised high into the air and then Garrison went to the ground. Farayne screamed in anguish. In mockery of her pain one of the men picked Garrison up and punched him sending him onto his back. The same man then picked him up and held him aloft so she could see the blood that flowed freely from his face. The men laughed and pointed to her, many climbing into the water to swim after her. Frantically grasping the small oar in the boat she paddled away as fast as she could, looking one last time at the only man she had ever truly loved. The last thing the lovely vampyre saw before the darkness of night swallowed her was her lover being viciously slammed onto a rock and his head cleaved from his shoulders as the jeers of the men followed her into shadow...

CHAPTER NINE
AMERICA

Farayne anxiously watched as the black of night gave way to the first fingers of dawn's caress. She had to get out of the boat but she was still yards from shore. The water was a brackish mixture of the harmless and of death so she could not swim for the shore.

"Ahoy, miss!"

Farayne looked up. Was the man talking to her?

"Ahoy!" Farayne had heard fisherman and sailors in other countries say that to each other as she and Garrison stepped off the ships they often traveled on. "Can you get me to shore?"

The young man pulled his boat up beside hers.

"Yes…or better yet, how about I simply help you into my boat, as I am traveling that way to drop off this net of fish I just caught?"

Farayne nodded eagerly and stood as the young man put his hand out to stop his boat from ramming her tiny craft. He offered his hand, after wiping it on his pants, and she stepped quickly into his boat, once again glancing up at the ever-lightening sky.

"Are you in a hurry, miss?"

Farayne had to think quickly.

"Yes sir…the sun, I am allergic. I did not expect my trip to take this long and I will be in dire straits if the sun touches me."

"Oh…I see. Well then let us get you to shore."

The young man was very strong and his bare arms bulged as he rowed as hard as he could toward shore.

"Miss, this is none of my concern, but why are you out so early in the morning, especially if you are allergic?"

Farayne once again had to think quickly. What on earth could she tell the young man? It was obvious that he was not prying but was simply very concerned about her. She spoke her answer as if it were the gospel truth and hoped that she would be convincing.

"I had to leave my home last night. There were evil men after me who wished me death for spurning their friend's advances.

They killed my husband after he put me in this boat. He stayed behind to keep them away from me and they murdered him right before my eyes. I had to flee without clothes, money…anything."

She almost felt guilty for lying, but her story was not *entirely* fabricated so she simply put what she had said out of her mind. The young man's eyebrows scrunched.

"I am sorry to hear that. Did you tell the authorities?"

Farayne shook her head.

"No, the man who made unwelcome requests of me was the Constable's son. It would have done no good."

The young man nodded as if he understood. Corruption in smaller towns was rampant. Farayne had often heard her former peers laughing about the dregs who were jailed for one frivolous reason or another. Many times after hearing their stories she came to the conclusion that the Constable's reasons for relieving them of what liberties they had were not valid and she often asked her father to intervene.

His answer was always the same.

"Farayne, you know that Constable Stone's reasonings for jailing those vagabonds was in the best interest of the town. Someone must keep those animals in line. They are nothing but rabid dogs otherwise!"

Farayne would always stamp her foot in anger and leave. She should have known that her father being such close friend with the Constable would have something to do with his sudden *blindness*. That angered her as, when her mother was alive, her father routinely championed the downtrodden and forgotten and was highly respected by all classes because of it. After her mother's death he'd become selfish and withdrawn, mocking and humiliating the poor people who'd once come to him for aid.

Those painful memories were brought back to the forefront as she and Garrison traveled the globe. Oftentimes she asked Garrison to intervene when they saw injustice, much the same as she had asked her father, but he too would not.

"Let it be, my queen. There is *nothing* you nor even I can do and we need *no* undue attention drawn to us," Garrison's voice softly chided inside her head.

Farayne suddenly snapped back to her present surroundings, which were becoming lighter. She panicked. The young man was looking at her.

"I do not have much I can give you, miss, but I have a small amount of money that I would be happy to part with for your benefit until you can take care of yourself."

Farayne looked at the man carefully. She was still in shock after seeing her love, her light and soul, murdered in front of her and so angry that she could not cry. A paralyzing numbness had overtaken her as the image of her husband's headless corpse on that rock replayed endlessly through her mind.

However, as much as she wished she could be, she could not be suspicious of this man. He seemed like an honest, hard worker with a genuinely kind spirit. How many men of his age, as he could not be more than Farayne would be were she still mortal, would be up before the dawn, to catch fish?

"But sir, if I take your money, what will you do? How will you live?"

The young man smiled.

"I am a fisherman, miss. I am used to being poor. If all else fails, I still have my fish that I catch for food and my wife bakes bread. We will be all right. She would be happier to know that I helped a stranger who needed it."

A tear slid down Farayne's cheek. Maybe there was hope for humanity after all.

"Thank you, kind sir, and I pray many blessings upon you and your wife's soul for being so charitable to me."

The boat suddenly hit the shore and Farayne was jolted almost pitching headlong over the side. The young man caught her in arms as powerful as her Garrison's and hoisted her up onto the soft dirt. Farayne turned to thank him again and he had his hand out. In his tightly clenched fist was a small satchel, which she surmised held the money he spoke of.

"Please, miss…take it."

Farayne hesitantly reached for the bag and with a curtsy hurried away as the sun began to rise.

Luckily for her, the town her little vessel had taken her to was right on the water, so she didn't have far to travel to seek safety. The town was large and she could blend in quite well until she could seek passage out at night.

Farayne hurried quickly into town. It was just coming to life it seemed. A man was beginning to blow out the lanterns that were still lit and people were milling about, some walking quickly, some talking and others sweeping and such. She wished she had more time to see this town and take in what it might have to offer her, but she did not. A building loomed to her left and she ducked quickly inside. Climbing the stairs in unladylike two-steps at a time fashion she just escaped the sun's lethal grasp. Once securely sheltered on the third floor of the old building, she rifled through the bag. The room was dark, very dark but her eyesight was accustomed to the darkness and she saw the bag as plainly as if she were seeing it in the light.

The coinage that spilled out onto her skirt as she dumped the bag was in pathetically small amounts. The more Farayne saw of life outside her born station, the more she came to realize just how unfair it truly was to those who worked hard. Those who slaved away their youth with backbreaking work would do anything to help others. They had nothing but were willing to share that 'nothing' with a total stranger. The people like her father and former peers who had never worked one day in their lives had more wealth than they could ever hope to spend, but would not drop even one coin on the ground for a starving child. It sickened her. In the grand scheme of things the hard workers were much more blessed and their souls pure, while those like her father had to donate large sums of money to the church to ease their conscience. But Farayne was not so blind that she did not realize that having money meant no worries. While rich in Heavenly rewards was a wonderful thing, as eternity was forever, poor in life on earth could be hell unto itself.

She fingered each coin, feeling guiltier than ever for taking what could amount to food, other than fish and bread, on the young man's table. The jeweled pin in her hair was worth more than what he'd given her! However the offer had been from his heart, was genuine and Farayne prayed that if there was any form of justice in life, any form at all, the man, whose name she did not even know, would be blessed in more ways than he could count.

Farayne put the coinage back in the well-used satchel and closed her eyes. She was hungry but that would have to wait.

CHAPTER TEN
A NEW LIFE FOR FARAYNE

Farayne was not a woman to be stopped if she wanted or needed something and getting to America would be no different. Being a beautiful and clever girl came in handy; she used her astounding looks and the fine money she made from the sale of her elegant hair pin to book her way onto a ship bound for America. She booked herself as the royalty she was born and due to her dress, manners and looks no one questioned her.

She was not accosted for the most part. The captain treated her to a fine cabin and as much privacy as he could. He was smitten with her, all men who crossed her path were it seemed, but no man held her interest unless they could serve some purpose for her.

Only one scalawag met his end while traveling with her. That was not bad odds considering that the entire ship was full of men. She arrived in America, leaving the ship in the middle of the night in the midst of a cold, January storm.

Farayne's attention was snapped back to her surroundings, the gurgling of her fountain a soothing reminder of where she was. She had so much that she still wished to remember...so much that she wanted to reflect upon. She had to hurry...

Farayne wandered alone for many years. Life and certainly not eternity were worth living any longer, it seemed. As time continued on and the ages of old gave way to new times, people became barbaric and rude, boorish and self-serving, no matter their class. She was lost without her love and killed many humans during her wanderings. Revenge, sweet, sweet revenge would be hers to dole out for the cruel injustice her husband had suffered at the hands of the men who were no more than the rabid dogs her father had spoken so carelessly of many, many years ago. They deserved to die and those that she did not kill quickly, she used them for food, enjoying slowly draining the life from them.

The men of the town, the lowlife cowards who had so immensely enjoyed her love's death and found her heartache so amusing suffered their fate as well. It took her a while, but she returned to the land of her birth and made certain that their suffering would be whispered about for many years to come.

Farayne looked around as the night air rustled her cape. The land had changed immensely and it barely resembled the home she had once known. The first place she went was to the Dancing Dragon Pub. All eyes locked on her as she walked in, but she paid them no mind. She recognized no one and her heart sank. Had it been *that* long? *It had been twenty years* and not only the crowd had changed, but even the bartender was different. What had she expected? While she lived forever and would wander all eternity watching the world change, those of mortal design died or moved on. She sauntered up to the counter.

"Bartender, what happened to the other man who used to own the tavern?"

"He moved away fifteen years ago and then died shortly after he moved. He was in poor health so he sold the pub to me and now I own it. Jansyn Pithlow, at your service."

Farayne smirked at him.

"There was a woman here at one time, 'Tansy the Trollop' they called her. Whatever became of her?"

"Why would you wish to know of a whore like her? Her escapades at this place are still spoken about to this day!"

Everyone at the bar laughed.

Farayne tossed her head in spoiled rebuff.

"My business is none of yours. Do you know what became of her or not?"

The man sniffed and set a pint down on the counter for a rough and filthy man who ogled Farayne with a disgusting glare.

"She died nearly twenty years ago. That is all I know. Now, do you wish something to drink or are you here only to waste my time?"

Farayne tossed her head and walked out. She wiped tears as she stood outside what once was the only escape she had from her doldrum life. She stared long and hard at the old building with its new thatched roof and timbers and for a moment, she could see Aggie in the corner, smoking her pipe and Tansy laughing with the men that she would later service.

She wished she'd been able to tell Tansy goodbye and wondered if the old harlot thought of her before she died. Farayne would never forget her and the lessons she helped her learn.

The next stop for Farayne was her former home with Garrison, though nothing was left of it. A new large and elaborate home stood on the ground where she and her beloved husband's manor once had. The land around it was still untouched for the most part, but this was *her* home, *her* land and it was gone. She could no longer become physically ill, but the sight of the land where her home once stood, housing another abode, made her heartsick. She stumbled away into the forest and hoped that she would find Aggie's grave undisturbed. There indeed would be hell to pay if something had happened to *her* final resting place.

Farayne enjoyed the night and it seemed that little had changed about Clark Forest, which was a welcome surprise for her.

She emerged on the other side of the thickly wooded land and as if a beacon shining to her on a stormy sea, Aggie's cottage appeared. Farayne squealed with glee and ran toward it but that

138

happiness was short lived. The cottage was abandoned, obviously for a while and had fallen into terrible disrepair. Farayne tried the door and it nearly fell to the ground. She stepped inside and looked around. Once again for a moment, she could feel the warmth of the fireplace, smell the tantalizing aroma of Aggie's blend of tobacco and it gave her a comfort that she'd not felt in ages.

"Aggie, you won't mind if I come back here and spend the night while I am visiting, will you?

The beautiful vampyre almost expected to hear her witch answer her and in a way she did. The wind picked up and leaves swirled at her feet.

"I didn't think you would."

Farayne walked out into the night in search of Aggie's grave and found it still intact but over grown. The roses and herbs she planted had taken over and though the area smelled divinely it was a forlorn sight.

"I have nothing better to do this night," Farayne whispered as she took off her cape and began pulling weeds, herbs and moving rose branches.

Farayne stopped as the wind shook her violently and she looked up. The night was returning to sleep and dawn was making herself seen.

"Thank you, Aggie."

Farayne looked at her night's work. She had completely cleaned out the area where her witch was laid to rest and was very proud. She decided that she would take the herbs she'd so carefully cultivated and leave them with the woman who now occupied the place where her home once sat. *She had kept the area up, it was attractive and maybe she could use them* Farayne mused silently. It would be a fitting reward for her.

Farayne had little use for humans any longer so she did not understand why she felt the need to be kind to them, but she caught herself occasionally doing nice things, such as offering a few year's worth of herbs to a stranger.

Farayne hurried back to the cottage and her timing could not have been better. The moment she ran through the door, her cape caught the first tinges of bright light.

She huddled in a dark corner under her cape and slept...

Farayne's blue eyes snapped open. It was already night and the sleep had done her good. She looked around Aggie's cottage once more before standing and stretching.

"Now to find something to tie these herbs with."

Farayne found an old length of cloth that she used to bundle the pungent spices and wrapping her cape around her once again, set off into the night.

She walked with purpose to the home of the family who now lived on the land she and her Garrison had once occupied. There was a little boy outside playing with some wood. As Farayne approached he stood up and looked frightened at seeing her.

"Do not fear me little boy. I come bearing gifts. Does your mother cook?"

The little boy brushed a red curl from his freckled forehead.

"No my lady, the cook does."

A cook? Farayne laughed. It was obvious that the family was well-to-do.

"Well of course she would, if she is the cook! You are a smart one. Your parents must be very proud. Tell me...does the cook use herbs?"

140

The boy nodded again, his bright mass of red curls bobbing effervescently.

"Yes, she uses many herbs."

Farayne stepped closer and handed the little boy the bundle. "Very well. Then take this to her with the compliments of Lady Farayne Gleneden-Maxwell."

The child took the bundle of herbs and walked to the house. He turned to thank the strange lady and found that she had disappeared. As quickly as she came, she had ebbed back into shadow...

Farayne's thoughts were much darker as she approached her next destination. She heard voices coming from within the old stone building and stopped to listen. She looked up and for a moment her eyes caught sight of the large cross atop the church. Her ears once again picked up voices, manly voices. She faintly recognized them all. They sounded much older than she remembered them from the night they ruined her life, but they were still the same. She would never forget their sound.

Blackness shrouded everything in an ebon cloak...as if it knew that she was coming to lay a long-sought vengeance to rest. Farayne charged up the steps and threw open the heavy oak door that shielded the men. The voices stopped and the men looked her way.

"This is a private meeting, my child. Come to service on Sunday and we will pray for your soul then."

Farayne smirked. "Such arrogance! I see that time has done nothing to slake your greed for power."

The man looked at the young woman with a cruel eye.

"Child, you are in the house of God."

"Oh am I now?" Farayne rudely interrupted. "And does God know that you murder innocent people whom you claim to be evil when you do not give them the opportunity to defend themselves against such charges?"

The man's mouth fell open. Farayne could see it and she relished it. She burned the image of his panic-stricken face into her mind's eye. Even though he was clearly frightened he continued his masquerade of innocence.

"Do I know you, child?"

Like venom dripping from the fangs of a snake, Farayne spat her answer at him…at all of them.

"Indeed you do. You murdered my husband twenty years ago. You came to our house -- the lot of you -- with a ghastly mob that burned our home to the ground and then you chased us to the dock. My husband put me in a small boat and set me afloat while you surrounded him and cut off his head. Oh yes, you know me and tonight you will know me a little better than you wish to!"

The Bishop's eyes grew wide and terrified and the other men, some old and frail by the passing of the years, tried to escape but Farayne was on top of them before they could get very far. She ripped each of their throats out but saved the Bishop for last. Blood-soaked and her eyes glowing with an unholy hatred, she slowly approached the trembling man.

"Bitch! Whore of hell! I knew we should have followed you into the water that night and made away with you while we could!" Farayne smiled, a malicious and evil smile, the kind of smile that made the terrified Bishop wet himself.

"Yes, you should have. Now you will not get the chance to. My husband and I were good people. We helped those in the community when you would not. We saved many homes and fed and clothed many downtrodden while all you did was fatten your purses. I shall take all that money tonight; I shall take it and distribute it where it should be…with those that truly need it. Then I will burn this church to the ground."

The Bishop laughed but it was not with a confidence he truly felt.

"You will not touch the house of God."

Farayne laughed loudly.

"This…this *building* is *not* the house of God. God would not condone such blasphemy within His walls."

Though never a religious person, Farayne had listened to and applied Aggie's own mixture of earth based religion and Christianity and it had often brought her comfort over the years.

Aggie was a Godly woman yet she still respected the Creator's hand in all around her where others did not see such

142

appreciation. She could stand with the best of those who used religion for their own gain…and take them down with that same religion.

With strength it did not look like she could possess, she jerked the trembling Bishop to his feet. He neither pleaded for his life, nor did he pray. He simply wept silent tears. They rolled down his face and onto his robe.

"May you burn in hell, you bastard!"

The blood tasted good as it slid down her throat…

Farayne had always hated the smell of inferior oil. Of course the men of the church, as they made themselves rich on the money their loyal and truly god-fearing parishioners gave them, and clothed themselves in the finest of silks, would not even purchase decent oil to light the church lamps with.

As she suspected, the coffer of money had been quite easy to find. It was right in the Bishop's office in a locked box. He was genuinely too arrogant, too bold to think that anyone would dare steal from him. She simply tore the box apart to relieve it of the precious money and now it sat at the back of the church waiting to be whisked away and back into the hands of those who deserved it. No one was about, to stop her, so her revenge would be sweet and oh so relished. Maybe once she righted the wrong from so long ago, Garrison's disembodied head would stop haunting her dreams.

She poured the last of the oil on the wooden pew in the front and took a candle down from atop the altar walking to the back. With one final glance around at the bloodied floor, walls and pews of the church, littered with the corpses of those she'd sought out. She smiled.

She opened the door, tossed the candle behind her onto the oil-laden floor and jumped to the dirt below so the flames would not follow her out. She laughed at the thought of the oil jumping the steps to get her, but as with the oil, the Bishop bought inferior candles too, not the nice beeswax candles that burned for hours and hours so the candle would do nothing more than what she wished it to. The flames rushed to the front of the church, the entire building succumbing to the less superior agents the catalysts were made from. The candle she used to light the church into an inferno was reduced to a burning puddle on the floor.

Farayne had to act quickly. Though the people of the town had nothing, they would give all they had and use all they had to save a false icon, *God's house* as the Bishop had so mistakenly frightened them into thinking. God would not live with swine, at least not the type of swine who took from innocent people and condemned those different from them. The God she knew from Aggie's teachings was a kind and loving being who saw no differentiation from one person to another and had no use for money, preferring to walk the streets and help rather than hoard for Himself.

Whether they realized it or not, she'd done this town a favor.

She set the heavy coffer down and opened the lock the Bishop had so generously left filled with the key. The lid popped open with a loud *clank* and she lifted it to be greeted by a nearly blinding flash of gold, silver and copper pieces, a few jewels and even what must surely be treasured family heirlooms.

She stood and brushed off her dress.

"You will now go back to those to whom you belong."

"Oy! What 'er you doin?"

Farayne looked up to see a haggard and obviously very tired man approaching, a water filled bucket with in his hand. He was barefoot and his clothes were disheveled. She was certain he'd jumped right out of bed to save his beloved church.

Farayne smiled, flashing pointed teeth and in a moment, had the man by the collar, her glowing eyes causing him to cry out in abject terror.

"Please, miss!"

"Silence!"

Farayne turned the man's head from side to side and looked him up and down.

"Yes, you will do. You will deliver a message to this town. I have liberated you from the corpulent greed-mongers who have stolen what appears to be this town's wealth…*your treasured belongings.* Your love of God cannot be measured by how much you give Him, for He has no need of money. You will see that this coffer's contents are properly re-distributed, that each member is to receive a fair share and the heirloom pieces be returned to their rightful owners."

The man nodded as best he could, his head in the vampyre's vise-like grip.

"I will be watching you and if you do not carry out my orders *exactly* as I say to, I will visit you…*at home.*"

The man nodded again and closed his eyes.

When he opened them, she was gone…

CHAPTER ELEVEN
TWILIGHT

Farayne once again set sail for America. She wandered aimlessly, the nights blurring, each new year just a continuation of the old one, decades passing into decades, everything warping into a sick parody of what once had been, changing her thoughts and heart until her desire to leave life for those who actually cared to live it, nearly consumed her.

The few humans she found to be good-hearted and worth saving heartened her, but they were not enough to quell her hatred for them. Those that she chose to spare were becoming fewer and farther between. If she could have, she'd have drunk dry her path through those that took their existence for granted, but she simply could not. There would be no one left. Her distaste for humans was so deep-seeded that she felt nothing for them any longer, absolutely nothing.

Tired of wandering and murder, Farayne settled in Orlando, Florida opening a nightclub, The Twilight Innocent. The money she took from her last lover, a very wealthy man who'd made the mistake of striking her in anger one evening after a week of partying and drugs, served her needs for a while.

The year was 2000. As many had so inaccurately predicted, the world hadn't come to an end. Before she opened the club, she worked the graveyard shift as an answering service operator just to have something to do, but she hated it. Her co-workers were gossips, her boss rude and demanding, not to mention he had wandering eyes and his hands tended to follow. So many times she envisioned herself ripping his throat out...not that she thought anyone would care. His lackeys might have, but she doubted that the people who were there to genuinely earn a paycheck would.

Her cubicle partner was a religious nut who eagerly awaited the onset of Y2K and end of the world as she swore it was going to be. In a way, Farayne shared the woman's zeal for an end. She had no use for the bitch's 'burn sinner burn' attitude, but an end was welcome.

However, Y2K came and went and the day was like any other. Her computer, as her doom and gloom co-worker told her it would, never crashed. She went outside at midnight and waited for the brimstone that she expected to fall from the sky, the earthquakes that would rip the streets to shreds and topple the buildings, crushing all within them, and the plagues that would consume her where she stood, but they didn't happen either. The prophesied and supposed biblical apocalypse never happened.

To a degree she actually was disappointed. Her life was humdrum and predictable, which was not bad, but she wished for something more. She didn't have much desire to do anything it seemed. She came home from work, watched television, drank the blood from the many packages of raw hamburger meat she bought, and then cooked the meat for an elderly neighbor who didn't have much money to spend on food. The woman never could figure out why her *young* neighbor was so generous, but she never questioned her. Farayne had forced herself to once again, give up human blood. Unless her life was in danger and it was necessary to defend herself she would not deviate. She had no desire drink from humans…not ever again.

Once Y2K passed and she was left to continue walking the life her world had become, she opened the club to seven days a week, from the weekend only status it previously held. She catered to every strange human in the central Florida area. People drove for miles to listen to live bands, dance and drink and it seemed that her club was full to capacity every night. Soon, her own kind began to seek her out, and eventually the club became a safe haven for every creature of the undead.

She loved seeing all the humans intermingling with the undead, unbeknownst as to what they stood beside, danced with, accepted drinks, a light for a cigarette, or affection from. She hoped that all the creatures, most vampyres and lycanthrope, but there were a few zombies and shape shifters as well, would exercise good taste to keep suspicion from her club. However, she had no way to be certain that they would take such precautions nor did she care to be. Who was she to condemn or condone? Her past was hardly laudable so she had no right to judge anyone else and how they conducted themselves.

If something *was* to ever happen and she found herself at odds with local law enforcement -- as quickly as she came, she would disappear, maybe back to Europe if she could manage it. She'd always felt more at home amongst castles and countrysides than she ever had amongst high rises and pollution.

So far the very large bouncers she'd hired kept the fighters, (as vampyres and lycanthropes were always prone to do) away from each other. She never had much trouble from the humans and did, to a degree, feel sorry for them. They thought themselves so superior, so chic and so desirable, yet they really had no clue how magnanimously pathetic they were. The royalty at the club were the vampyres, followed by the warrior lycanthropes and then lastly the suave and debonair zombies who seemed amused by not only both vampyres and lycans, but by the amusing fakery and bullshit antics of the humans. The shapeshifters didn't care for anyone from *any* class of undead and seemed interested in only one thing...fucking with the human's frail minds They spent night after night having fun at the expense of the unsuspecting "one-dimensions," as the shapeshifters called them. Thanks to their trickery, her club had gotten the reputation for being haunted, which brought even more business to her. The shapeshifters were carefree and happy to do what they wished in a world they felt was at their feet. In a way, Farayne admired and envied them. They had not one care, not one worry...they simply did as they wished.

She rolled the young man off her. He'd tried to rob her as she left the club before sunrise.

"I hope it was worth it, asshole."

She laughed loudly. He tasted good, better than she thought he would. *Maybe she could learn to like human blood again? No...that was silly. Blood was blood...*she shook her head and looked around as the sun began to rise. She was tired. Existence had been unbearable the past centuries she'd seen the world grow and change and it would be so easy to simply let the sun consume her. The thought had paraded itself in her mind more than once and all the times it had, she chased it, rationalized it and then ultimately given up on it, fearful of what awaited her at the end.

Though many men vied for her hand over the centuries, she'd used all of them. They were sex and nothing more to her. Requests for dates were laughed off, but she fed her physical needs with any man who would fall into under her spell. She didn't care if what she did was wrong; she cared only for herself. Without her Garrison to tend to her and fulfill her wants and desires, who else would do it? Though Farayne enjoyed her new life in Orlando, and all the new friends she made she never forgot her Garrison, her eternal love and never loved again.

She could feel the warmth of the day now. The sun was not fully in the sky yet, but it would be only a matter of moments. As she'd done so many times -- the same scenario that all too often played out for her -- she backed out on the wish to kill herself. She did wish to die, but she wished it to be by someone else's hand and in as quick a manner as possible. She pulled the man's coat from him and covered up as best she could, hurrying home before the sun could harm her.

Farayne leaned heavily against the door. She'd just made it home. It wasn't that she was intentionally trying to kill herself, at least not consciously intentionally if that made any sense, but she really was so tired of 'fighting' every day.

She'd lived a long life, she'd done more things in her years of existence than most people would in two or three, she'd lived her dreams, cried rivers of tears, been to the top of the mountain and had sunken to the depths of despair. She had nothing keeping her in her present life and she had nothing to prove. Didn't she deserve a break?

She looked at the shafts of sunlight beckoning her to that blessed eternal sleep. She looked harder. Were they beckoning her or taunting her?

She pushed herself away from the door and looked at the shiny death all around her. It would be so easy to just step into a ray of release and allow it to carry her away, it really would.

She shrugged the coat off that protected her on her journey home and simply stood, watching the beams of light dance all around her. She had mirrors in her house because she loved to look at herself. Judging by the stares and catcalls she got each night to and from the club, it was obvious that others enjoyed looking at her too. This particular morning though those reflective glass pools could prove to be her bane if one picked up a beam of light and threw it back at her.

She laughed.

Stepping out into the foyer of her neat little home she put her hand out to one of the enticing rays. She allowed it to settle on her and she waited. It was only mildly hot at first and then the pain grew in intensity until she jerked it away from the molten torment, crying out. She looked at her smoking, hole-infested appendage. It began to heal right in front of her eyes. She sighed and then smiled. At least if she decided that she couldn't take the doldrums of living any longer, her death would be a quick one. She could endure the pain as long as the eternal rest that followed was quick.

Suddenly she felt renewed. Not even bothering to sidestep the rays of warm fire that wished to consume her, she waltzed to her bedroom, the burning of a thousand knives stabbing into her pale skin.

CHAPTER TWELVE
THE FINAL ACT

The darkness of the office seemed to close in on her as she sat once again at her computer. She was lost in thought and reminiscing. She found that she often did so, thinking of times past and people she'd loved…people she missed and always would. Tansy, Aggie and the others flashed briefly in her mind again and she shook her head as if physically shaking them from her thoughts. She'd done enough reflecting…at least for this night. The reflections were almost painful this time. Well that was not actually so, they were always painful. She hated to put herself through the anguish that seemed to haunt her every step, tap her on the shoulder and dare her to forget it. But she couldn't forget it and would continue to torture herself.

No matter how hard she tried she simply could not wrest her heart from the images that plagued her every waking minute. She gently swished the glass of fresh blood in her goblet. She didn't think about where it came from, she didn't think about what she had to do to obtain it; and how she'd broken her promise to herself, she simply drank it and allowed the sustenance to infuse her body with much needed nourishment. She was definitely tired...tired of this life. So long she'd lived in this manner, so long she'd wracked her brain with images and memories of things that could not be changed…things she'd done. How much longer could she do this to herself? How much longer *would* she do this to herself?

The tears started again and she wiped them quickly away. No amount of tears, no amount of regret, no amount of atonement would change her past. She got up from her desk and walked over to the window in her office, watching the bodies writhe on the dance floor below her. The line stretching around the block before the club even opened would be a welcome sight to any other club owner, and while she was pleased, it gave her no real joy. Days and nights…except for the light, was there any difference?

A knock woke her from her sad daydream.

A burgundy head of hair with a pale face and heavy, black lined eyes poked its way into her office.

"Farayne, can I come in?"

Farayne nodded and smiled. It was Trish, her friend and confidant...the only real friend she'd had since Aggie. Trish walked in, closing the door behind her, her tall and thin velvet and lace-clad body settling lightly in a velvet covered chair.

"Trish, I'm tired, tired of everything."

The pretty young vampyre rolled her eyes.

"Here we go again. Whatever do you mean, Farayne? *How could you be tired?* Number one, you can't physically be tired. It's just not possible and if you are talking about tired of living, *again*, you are just being ungrateful. You have everything any woman could ever want!"

Farayne sighed.

"I may seem ungrateful in your opinion, Trish, but you haven't lived as long as I have, either. You haven't seen what I've seen nor endured what I have. There may come a time somewhere in the future where living forever becomes too great...even for a vivacious little sprite like you. I'm just restless, restless and tired of not having my Garrison by my side. He would have loved this era. He would have loved the music, the clothing. He was elegant but he was always one for something new and adventuresome."

"You need to find a new love."

"No."

"But Farayne!"

Trish rolled her eyes again, her voice clearly exasperated. It was the same thing every single time she mentioned finding romance to the ancient vampyre.

"No. That matter is not up for discussion, Trish. There will never be another Garrison. He was a dream. His mannerisms and everything about him were impeccable. He was a gentleman, he was a wonderful lover, husband...and if we ever could have had children, I would have loved to see what kind of father he would have been. I'm certain he would have been an excellent one. Men like Garrison do not exist any longer and haven't for quite some time. All I have for the male species now is disgust. They are nothing but pigs. They're emotionally immature, needy and all they

152

care about is getting a woman into bed for a fast fuck. They are rude, boorish and can't carry on a decent conversation. Honestly, Trish, have you heard some of the language these men use?"

Trish grinned, "Like your potty mouth miss, 'I am eloquent and can out orate anyone in town, but I have a mouth like a sailor when I wish to'?"

Farayne grinned. It was true. She'd picked up some very bad habits in her more recent years and having a terribly vile mouth was one of them.

"Say what you wish, I have no desire to ever love again if those *things* that are called men are what I have to choose from."

Trish laughed.

"Oh, Farayne you are too picky, I mean honestly too picky. Do you really think that *all* men are worthless?"

Farayne shrugged.

"Maybe in *your* eyes I am too picky. *I* don't think so. My opinion of men is not a high one so I won't settle for just anything. I know what I want and I have yet to find it."

Farayne's words were clipped as if she wished to speak no more on the subject. But she knew that with Trish a conversation was never truly over until there was absolutely nothing left to say.

"You just want another Garrison, Farayne, and you will never find him, not in this time. He was a once in a lifetime love."

Farayne knew that Trish was right. She didn't care. Most humans could only hope for, at the most, even if they married very young, eighty years with their mates. She hadn't spent as much time as she wished with her Garrison before his demise, but they'd loved each other enough for an eternity. That was good enough for her. She was thankful for the time she spent with him and counted herself very fortunate.

Suddenly all fell silent. It seemed that Trish was weary of arguing with her friend and Farayne was just as weary of speaking...

Blaring lights woke Farayne from her daydream. Trish was loudly popping her gum and on her cell phone and she was back in front of her computer, each of them going about their own business. The disc jockey, "DJ Sanitorium Sanctimonium" he called himself, was telling everyone that it was time to go. Farayne would be leaving soon but before she did, she had something that she'd decided to do, something to work on that she'd toyed with for ages and Trish didn't need to see it…yet. Wasn't she ever going to leave?

"I'm out of here, Farayne. I'll see you again tonight!"

Farayne smiled. Had Trish read her mind?

"Okay."

Farayne turned back to her computer and touched the mouse. The castle and adjacent cemetery of the computer façade disappeared, replaced by an official document. Her fingers began nimbly moving across the keys. It would be done soon and she could go home. It was the quiet of pre-dawn, after the club closed that she cherished because she could think, she could plan and she could then put those well executed thoughts into action with no prying.

The door opened.

"Oh…Farayne, you're still here. I apologize. I would have never simply walked in had I known you were still here."

"Yes, Jeffrey I am still here and will be for a while. I know that you had no way to see me in here. Go on, go home and thank you for keeping the peace. I'll lock up when I leave."

"Farayne, are you okay?"

Not a man of many words, her burly bouncer's concern was touching.

"I am fine, Jeffrey, now go home."

"As you wish, boss. Good morning."

"Good morning."

The bouncer closed the door and Farayne smiled. Many times she'd watched Jeffrey work and never could get over how agile he was to be so muscular.

She went back to her computer screen and the document in front of her. She sent it to her printer and waited…

Farayne locked up the club. She really was tired. Trish meant well and she was charismatic in her own way but she'd crossed over only seventy-five years previously. She was a mere child! What could she possibly know, what could she possibly

154

understand about how life was for Farayne and her Garrison? Farayne could explain all day and night, she could paint as many articulate mental pictures for her friend as possible, but unless someone had actually lived through such elegant, albeit difficult times, there was no way they could truly grasp how things once were.

How Farayne wished that she could go back, even if for just one night to what she'd once lived. It was not so much that she missed that life but that she left so many things unsaid, so many things that would have made a difference, to her father, to what few friends she had. If nothing else, even if she never spoke to any of them again, her father included, at least it would have been closure. She'd sought out her father's grave after his death, finding him buried on their ancestral property instead of in the churchyard, beside her mother, as she always suspected he would be.

Fortunately, her former home had become a tourist attraction and was open to the public. Otherwise, she might have never been able to see her father's final resting place. She wept bitterly as she caressed his stone, much to the strange and confused looks of those around her. She didn't care. She chose as late an hour as she could to visit the estate and swathed head to toe in white to protect her, she ignored the burning of the day's dying rays as she bade her father a final, tearful farewell.

Farayne's thoughts turned to Garrison as she pulled on the lock securing the gate.

"Garrison, Garrison," she whispered, turning to the east. The moon was going to rest…she didn't have much time.

Now here she was, walking amongst her favorite roses, her mental journey back through time and on the path her life had taken, come to an end. She closed her eyes and breathed in the tease of the early morning at her nose. In such peaceful silence, she could hear her fountains gurgling and the babbling of the small, shallow brook that ran in her backyard. She had already fed her bright orange carp, bidding them farewell and swishing her hand in the water in a final gesture. There was nothing more to do now but wait.

As she figured, when she called Trish, she hadn't been home. Probably out getting laid or scoring a meal or both, knowing her. Farayne laughed. Her message had been short and to the point, "I have something I wish to give you. It will be in my backyard on the table. Come by before you head to the club so you can get it."

Her home was secluded and she loved it. It had taken her quite a while to find the perfect piece of property…the perfect setting. She had a beautiful little cottage, custom built after her beloved witch, Aggie's cottage, on the land and then set about making it hers in every conceivable form.

She sat down on her favorite cast iron chair, clutching the ancient talisman that hung from her neck. It had been a gift that her only true friend had given her upon her wedding day and Farayne had never, not since Aggie placed it around her neck, taken it off. She'd made many friendships over the centuries and even a few close ones after moving to Orlando and opening the club, but none had the effect on her life that Aggie's had…not even Trish's.

She looked up and smiled. She thought at first when her decision became final and she began setting things in motion that she might miss this life. But she knew now that she really wouldn't. Trish would enjoy owning the club and Farayne knew the vivacious vampyre, who'd completely embraced her free lifestyle, living each night to the fullest, would find someone to buy her home, someone who would appreciate all she had done…and take care of her beloved carp for her. She fingered the envelope, containing her Will, freshly printed from the printer at the club, and the deed to the club and her house.

Farayne looked again at her dress, the light and airy fabric clinging to her shapely body. Trish always scolded her for buying second-hand clothes when she could afford the best that any fine shopping excursion to New York City could offer. The truth was that Farayne loved her second hand clothes and she loved the variety she could gain from shopping the way she did. Aggie had always dressed simply and Farayne did too.

The sky became lighter, the gray of the overcast pre-dawn, giving way to the pale orange of the morning. It was almost too warm now, but that was to be

156

expected. She really had missed that after her crossing, the warm sun on her face as she explored the countryside of her home.

Home...home, she had never had another home...not since the manor she had expected to spend the rest of eternity in had burned to the ground right before her horrified eyes. She'd never felt at home in her father's house. She'd found a haven in Orlando, but her home would always be with her love, in their country manor. She smiled again as her skin began to smoke. She closed her eyes.

"I'm coming, my love. It won't be long. I'll be with you soon."

ABOUT THE AUTHOR

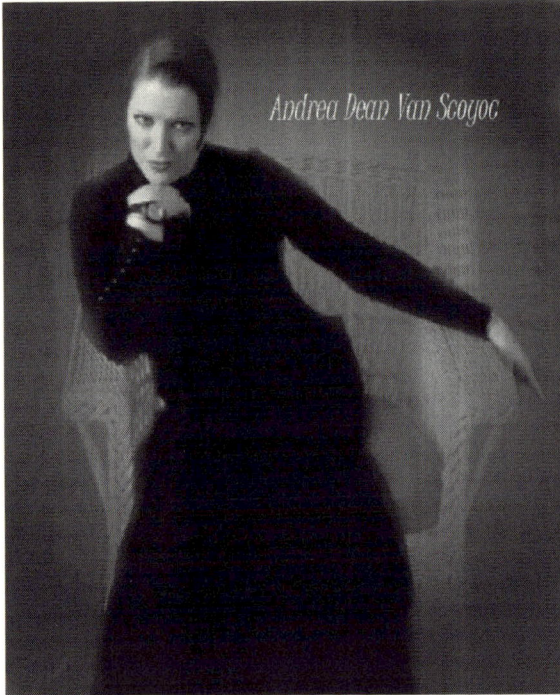

Andrea Dean Van Scoyoc

Called "One of the most unique and twisted authors of our generation," Andrea Dean Van Scoyoc is a best selling, award winning author of Horror Sinisteria.
From the twisted to the paranormal, from the Occult to pirates, Andrea can write it, write it well and keep her fans and critics begging for more.
A force of nature, Andrea has blazed a path through a genre most often dominated by men. She is routinely sought out for appearances at everything from private functions to public venues to conventions, where she appears as a celebrity guest.
Please visit Andrea online at
http://thelosttheforgottenthedamned.com/ or visit her at one of her many appearances she makes during the year. She doesn't bite…very much.

FALLEN   VAN SCOYOC